MOON BLOOD

The First Blood Son

Book 3

Carol McKibben

www.trollriverpub.com

Moon Blood
The First Blood Son (Book 3)
Copyright © 2018 Carol McKibben
ISBN: 978-1-946454-58-4

Cover design: Uniquely Tailored
Cover Images supplied by: Faestock https://www.deviantart.com/faestock
Photo by Matt Benson on Unsplash Moon
Editors: Ravi Banthia, Stephanie McKibben

Join the fun with Author Carol McKibben for giveaways, updates and new release opportunities at:

http://eepurl.com/bAuq2b

Other books by Carol McKibben:

<u>The Snow Blood series:</u>

Snow Blood: Season 1

Snow Blood Season 2

Snow Blood: Season 3

Snow Blood: Season 4

Snow Blood: Season 5

Kane:
The First Blood Son (prequel of the Snow Blood
series)

<u>The First Blood Son series:</u>

Moon Blood: The First Blood Son series (Book 1)

Moon Blood: The First Blood Son series (Book 2)

<u>Stand alone novels:</u>

Riding Through It

Luke's Tale

DEDICATION

For Debi Macmillan, my sister wolf

EPISODE ONE

NIGHTMARE

I awoke to pressure on my chest just as night descended. Invisible hands stroked my back and legs. I startled onto four paws, my claws digging into the bedding. The dark room where Kane, Zandra, and I slept gave no clue to an intruder. The air smelled bitter. Even though I was a vampire, and my body wasn't affected by heat or cold, a shift dropped the temperature so that puffs of breath from my low warning growl clouded to steam. The pressure of a presence lingered around me. Hands tried crushing me down.

Peering through the pitch black with my enhanced vision, I saw that my sire Kane struggled against something. He pushed his hands up as if something pressed down on him.

"No!" he shouted and jerked into a sitting position. His ankles bashed against one of the tall bed posts. I realized at once that what I had felt was not directed at me but to Kane.

Zandra, who now shared the bed with us during our daytime rest after our tumultuous battle with the berserker werewolves, bolted upright at the sound of her lover's voice. "What?" She rubbed her eyes and blinked at the first blood son of Brogio, the original vampire. "Was it a nightmare?"

"I don't have dreams or nightmares." Kane brushed a long strand of his dark-brown hair from in front of his brown eyes. Confusion spread across his strong chiseled facial features.

Zandra placed an arm around Kane's broad shoulders and pressed a cheek to his. "Tell us."

I lay down, crawled to his feet, and licked the top of one of them. Pressure descended upon me. I could feel hands on me.

Kane nodded at me as the automatic lights began to glow indicating that night was upon us.

"Something held me down... hovered... I was paralyzed. Fingers probed at me. Lips kissed me... everywhere." Kane ran his hands over his eyes. "I... pleasure... but fear at being so completely in the grip of another. When I opened my eyes..."

His abrupt halting of the story shot me a mental picture of beautiful Selene, Brogio's wife. Since Kane made me kindred, we have been connected. I feel what he does. I hear his thoughts as he does mine. This connection is advantageous, since I'm a female hybrid wolf and can't vocalize my thoughts.

I directed my opinion to him. You will never open your heart to Zandra because Selene still lives there.

He hesitated to continue to not reveal his unrequited love for a woman who was the light mirror image to Zandra's dark reflection. Where Selene's long hair is silver, Zandra's is silky brown. The shape of Selene's silver-blue eyes is the same as Zandra's golden orbs. Selene is fair. Zandra is olive skinned. Other than that, they have the same tall height and slender figure. Selene, once vampire, had been restored as a human like her husband, Brogio, the first vampire. Zandra, like Kane, is the first born, not of a vampire but of the original werewolf.

"What? What did you see?" Zandra pressed her strong fingers into Kane's arm as if to squeeze the answer from him.

He sighed. "A beautiful blonde woman who smiled at me. But then her face turned a demonic red, and her beautiful teeth became fangs. Bat-like wings sprung up from her back, and I felt talons dig into my arms and legs."

"My gods, what a nightmare. Anything else?" Zandra rubbed Kane's arm which showed no marks or signs of attack.

"Yes. She declared she would take my soul, but stopped. The smile faded from her horrible face, and she whispered a dawning realization."

"Whispered what?" Zandra leaned back to look at him.

Kane smirked. "She said, 'but you have no soul!'"

Zandra laughed. "Well, that's no big news." She took both her hands and rubbed his head, making a mess of his shoulder-length hair. "Okay, so you had a nightmare. You should interpret the monster as me and realize that the message is that we need to have more sex."

Kane joined in her laughter, and I relaxed a bit.

"Maybe," Zandra stood up on both knees revealing her naked body while mocking a menacing face, "you're afraid I'll go all werewolf on you in the middle of sex."

Kane grabbed her and tumbled her under him as they both screamed in laughter. Disgusted and not wanting to observe what I knew was coming, I jumped down from the bed, nudged the bedroom door open, and padded into the hallway. They might be able to laugh it off, but I could feel in my bones that something else was coming for him, for all of us.

∞

As I stepped into the night, Zandra's numerous brothers stood watch outside Kane's Tuscany wine estate chateau. They kept vigil to guard against a rogue band of werewolves who might try to take revenge on the slaughter we had dealt them the previous week. Kane had devised a clever plan to destroy thousands of berserker wolves dead set on destroying him, the new leader of the vampire nation. We expected retribution from other nations for the death of their Italian kindred.

All Zandra's brothers were large, hulking versions of her olive complexion and dark-brown hair and eyes. I spied Zeb, the eldest of the brothers, as I stretched my sleep away. He stood near a large cedar tree. Eyes that had previously held distrust now softened as he glanced at me. I had proven my affection for his sister, whom he loved above all others.

Zachary, the next eldest brother, slinked quietly toward me from the nearby vineyard.

He stopped just short of Zeb and grabbed a fly from the air and crushed it.

Zale followed, nodded, and grinned. His charm softened his ruggedness. "All quiet this day and night in the fields, Zeb."

"Don't state the obvious," Zeb quipped at his brother. He had no time or tolerance for charm.

Zale smiled and rubbed my head and then sat next to me on the ground.

Shy Zander joined us from the entrance gates to the estate, followed by Zeno and Zindel who caught up to him and poked fun at their quiet brother.

"It's a wonder Zander could see anything coming." Zeno jabbed his brother in the ribs.

"Yeah," Zindel rubbed the shy one's head, "he's always looking down at his feet."

Zander brushed his brothers away and scooted over to lean against the front door with arms crossed.

Zeno and Zindel were full of pride and fierce in battle. All the brothers were forces with which to be reckoned, but Zylon's appearance would terrify little children. He resembled Kane's descriptions of battle-scarred Vikings. He silently moved from behind the cedar tree and startled me. Second only to Zeb in size, I had watched him break enemies in half with his bare hands.

Zane's casual stroll from the forest reminded me of his deceptive demeanor. He appeared to not pay attention but became an obvious predator when the opportunity became available.

As Zohar and Zoltan joined us from the back of the estate, I thought how much alike all the brothers appeared, but how their difference in character was marked.

Zohar's nod as he approached was nonchalant and carefree. His inner spirit embraced freedom and fun.

Zoltan's sensitive eyes met mine as he grinned at me. I had liked him the moment we met. He was the baby of the family, and I knew him as the kind one and my favorite of the brothers.

The front door opened suddenly, and Zander fell backward.

Kane prevented Zander's fall by catching the shifter by his collar and glanced around at everyone. "Come inside and have a meal as my small thanks for your daylight vigil." He opened the door wide for all to enter.

As the brothers trudged past Kane and Zandra toward the dining room, Zohar threw out a suggestion. "I think we should attend the Lucca Summer Festival tonight. We need a break and some fun."

"Always the fun," Zeb grumbled. "Why expose ourselves to a public attack?"

"Berserkers aren't going to attack us in a public square," Zachary, the logical one, mumbled.

"Yes!" Zandra whirled around and gave Kane her best puppy-dog eyes. "What fun. I read this year Ringo Starr, Roger Waters, and King Crimson will perform in an all-star band."

We joined the group in the dining room just as James, Kane's silent and ever-present servant, set down a glass of human blood for his master and a bowl of the nectar on the floor for me.

I half listened as I lapped up what I considered to be God's gift. James stood next to me against the wall to make himself unobserved and waited for me to finish my meal.

"What I'd like to see," Kane quipped, "is Joe Perry and Alice Cooper team up with that pirate actor Johnny Depp." He swallowed his blood meal in two large gulps. "They're supposed to create 'Hollywood vampires' or so the advertisements say. Might be fun after the morbid days we've spent of late."

I licked my chops and sat back on my haunches. Finally, I had learned to control the euphoria that overcame me after drinking blood. In my earlier days as a vampire, that was not the case. In the beginning, gorging on human blood would almost knock me out.

James bent, picked up my bowl, and made himself scarce. An odd duck, his mild personality, medium build, and nondescript features fooled many into thinking he was harmless. People underestimated James at their own peril.

"Oh, yes. I'd love to see that." Zandra placed a quick peck on Kane's pale cheek and sat down to dig in to a breakfast of steak, bacon, eggs, potatoes, biscuits, and pancakes that would have choked a lumberjack.

"It is only a little over an hour's drive from here," Zachary mumbled with his mouth full of steak and bacon.

"I'll go only if Kane lets us ride in the limo," Zeb announced as he licked the grease from his fingers.

Kane smirked. "Do you actually think that all of you will fit in one car, limo included?"

Zachary interjected, "Would not the limo and the town car work? Kane, you can take Zandra and Moon in your sports car."

After a lot of boring banter, much of which I ignored, it was settled, and we were off. Despite the fun atmosphere everyone embraced, a growing fear gnawed at the bottom of my stomach. I shot Kane a mental message. I fear danger awaits us at this event. Let the brothers and Zandra go, and let's stay here.

Kane shot me a look. You worry too much. If danger awaits us, it will be met in kind.

I wondered if an evil he had yet to meet and overcome might take him by surprise.

∞

The festival music hurt my ears. I longed to return to Villa Chiantigiana, Kane's wine estate. To block out the blaring noise, I closed my eyes and thought of the place I now called home. I visualized its green, hilly panorama and vineyards, as well as the surrounding forest as far as the eye could see. As it was in the Chianti Hills, Kane said it was in the heart of Tuscany, just a short distance from Florence. Rows of ancient cypress trees lined either side of the long drive through the fields I loved to explore up to the estate house. The big nineteenth-century stone villa had a red-tiled roof. I was grateful that my vampirism had cured my color blindness.

My favorite game was to run past the fifteen bedrooms on the upper floors, leap down the circular staircase, scamper over the marble black-and-white entry, scoot through the hall out to the pool, and dive into the water. James failed to find this amusing, particularly when I shook off on Kane's beautiful dark-stained cypress wooden furniture in the den.

I also loved to explore the rooms that Kane ordered me not to disturb, like his large library and study or the laboratory filled with experiments at different stages that tickled my nose and made me sneeze. Sometimes after quenching my bloodlust, I'd climb to his rooftop balcony with a star-watching telescope or snoop through the inside of the many bedrooms filled with paintings and sculptures. I loved to roll around on his expensive antique rugs. Whenever James caught me, he would chase me down into the large den with a huge fireplace and a room-long bar. I longed to snooze by the fire in the den and relax, if just for a while.

Loud cheering startled me from my reflection. Kane and Zandra had split up from the brothers who each had found companionship with the local women who appeared enthralled with them.

Sitting next to Kane, I glanced at my sire and Zandra as they relaxed in front of the stage and focused on the vampire act. Still concerned for their safety, I wandered away through the crowd hoping to find a quiet place to observe them and watch the crowd. Before I had gotten some fifty feet, a large black wolf blocked my path. His iridescent green eyes held mine. The attraction between us surprised and distracted me from the shocked crowd surrounding us. As a hybrid wolf, I can pass as a white husky, much like my biological father, Snow Blood. But this full-blooded wolf caused quite a stir. Glancing around, I noticed people backing away as a dazzling woman emerged through the crowd.

Her approach was like one I might have in a dream. Her boots made no sound on the cobblestone street, and she appeared to glide rather than walk. I couldn't take my eyes from her. Long, wavy, red hair hung past her waist. Her piercing green eyes matched those of the wolf. Tight leather pants, a low-cut matching black vest, and knee-high boots covered her silky skin and flaunted her flawless curves. The men in the surrounding crowd appeared dumbstruck at the personification of female sexuality that she exuded, but the babies and young children began to scream.

Their cries shook me out of the trancelike effect she'd created on me. My hackles rose, and a shiver ran through my entire body.

She stopped and frowned at the wolf. "Samil, naughty boy. Thought I'd lost you." She glanced toward me, and I sensed feigned surprise. She stretched her hand out. "Whom have you discovered, Samil? How beautiful you are, my hybrid girl."

I shrank from her touch and backed away.

The black wolf called Samil moved with me and kept his shimmering eyes on mine all the while.

Kane's voice shot through my brain. Moon, where are you?

I am here, Master.

Kane parted the crowd and stopped dead in his tracks at the sight of the woman. "Selene?" He shook his head and blinked, trying to hide his shocked expression. He swayed and then steadied his body. The silence grew uncomfortable as my master's eyes locked with the stranger's. At last, he blinked again and appeared to break the woman's-controlled stare. "I'm sorry. I thought you were someone that I know."

I padded to my sire, ignored Samil's intense stare, and stood next to Kane.

The woman approached as the crowd around us began to dissipate. She held out her hand to my sire. "I am Lilith. This is my wolf Samil. We came across your lovely hybrid and thought to return her to her owner."

Kane smiled and took the woman's hand. "Kane de Medici, madam. Thank you for stopping to help my disobedient pet.

I cringed at the name calling, but shot a warning. Beware of this woman. She gives me the creeps.

Quiet, Moon.

I sat back on my haunches and wondered why an age-old vampire always appeared to be ruled by his mating desires.

As if on cue, Samil moved to sit next to me and lick my face.

He stood just as I did, and I searched his green eyes for some sign of danger. I saw conflicting good and evil in them and backed away.

Again, I warned. This is the danger I feared for us.

EPISODE TWO

ENCOUNTERS

Zandra pushed through the crowd and halted in her tracks at the sight of Kane who stood frozen in place while staring at Lilith. "Oh, thank goodness you found her."

Lilith swung her gaze at Kane's companion, and her eyes became slits of green assessment.

Zandra's golden orbs shot out a warning that I interpreted as "hands off."

The smell of malice assaulted my nostrils. I wouldn't want to get in the middle of a disagreement between these two. I imagined Zandra would wolf out, but something about this Lilith told me she'd hold her own.

The growing tension eased when a man with a T-shirt that read "Event Team" barged in among us. He pointed to the wolf. "It's been reported that this animal is causing a disturbance among the concertgoer. People are frightened. To whom does it belong?" He glanced among the humans in our group.

"Samil is with me." Lilith flashed him a smile that beguiled him. Lust combined with confusion spread across his face, and he stumbled for the right words. "Well, uh, would you mind taking him out of the... the plaza... miss?"

Lilith again smiled and took Samil by the collar. "Of course."

The man backed away with a red face. "Thank you."

Lilith then turned back to Kane with a dazzling smile.

Avoiding the possibility of introductions, Zandra grabbed Kane's arm, gave me a nod to follow back to the stage, and marched off with my sire who tried to wipe the grin off his face at his companion's obvious jealousy.

I followed but looked back to get another glimpse of the handsome wolf only to observe the two strangers had disappeared into the crowd. The moment they were no longer present, I felt relief.

"So, who are the woman and the wolf?"

Kane shrugged. "I don't know them, but the woman seems familiar somehow."

Like me, I could sense the release he experienced when they disappeared.

"Your interest in her made me a bit uncomfortable, Kane."

Kane threw back his head and burst into laughter. He lifted her off the ground, swung her around by the waist, and kissed her cheek. "You're most beautiful when you are jealous."

Zandra stomped her foot as he set her down. "I am not jealous! Don't you think at this point and your track record that I see danger around every corner? Someone or *thing* is always after you, either to destroy you or use you in some way."

Kane stopped, and the smile faded from his face. His question filled my head. *You felt the woman's pull on us, didn't you?*

Yes, and we were released when she disappeared.

He looked Zandra in the eyes. "My life as a vampire has always been about survival—to find food, to ward off attacks, to avoid the true death. But I asked for life eternal so that I could acquire knowledge. Since my days as an assistant to da Vinci and now with Elon Musk, I keep my sanity by learning and growing and surrounding myself with loved ones. If I live this life always on guard, always afraid, it won't be worth existing. It appears that the last few years, first with Brogio, Selene, and Snow Blood, and now with you, Moon, and your brothers, I have done nothing but fight for survival."

Zandra pushed a lock of his long, brown hair away from his cheek and stared up into his dark eyes. "That appears to be our plight."

"But one that I will take on when it comes my way instead of existing in fear. There's being smart, and then there's letting the past hold you back and preventing you from exploring all the possibilities of what can be." He pulled Zandra to his chest and wrapped his arms around her. "Trust me, if the woman and the wolf are a threat, we will deal with it soon enough. For now, let's do what we came here to do—enjoy ourselves."

I alerted just as Zeb and Zachary found us in the crowd.

"Kane," Zeb towered over my very tall sire, "I just spotted the new pack leader of the berserkers with two of his henchmen in the crowd."

Zandra grabbed her oldest brother's muscular arm. "That would be Matteo Ricci and his brothers Diego and Paolo. They have far-reaching relationships throughout Europe."

"And they didn't participate in the battles we had with their dead leaders." Zachary placed a large hand on his brother's broad shoulder.

"Only because the Italian flesh eaters preserve their designated survivors, much like when the Executive Branch of the American government assures that someone will be alive to rule when all the powers that be are gathered in one place."

Kane placed the arm not surrounding Zandra over the brothers' wide shoulders to bring them into a tight circle.

I pressed against his back legs and surveyed the crowd for approaching danger.

Zeno joined us before another word could be spoken. "Our brothers have followed them and have them cornered near the Puccini Museum."

Before anyone could respond, Zeno hastened through the crowd with Kane, Zandra, and her two oldest brothers behind them.

I weaved through legs, small children, and jumped over pet dogs to catch up with them just outside the throng in the plaza.

Traveling another one hundred paces or so, we found Zale, Zander, Zindel, Zylon, Zohar, and Zoltan surrounding three large berserkers with their backs to the wall of the museum.

Kane whipped around the brothers to face the potential threat. One of the three stepped in front of the one in the middle that I perceived as the Alpha. Alphas smell of strength that expands beyond the others.

The Alpha's guard opened his mouth, and his fangs extended.

Kane's eyes glowed red, and his fangs extended too.

I instantly appeared by Kane's side. I bared my teeth, saliva dripping from my mouth. My body tensed, ready to leap.

The largest of the three, the one I thought the Alpha, held out his hand. "I am Matteo Ricci. We mean no harm."

Zandra stepped forward on the other side of Kane.

"Diego," Matteo snapped, "step back unless you want the jaws of death to end you now."

Paolo, the other, clasped his brother's arm and pulled him back against the wall. "It's the bloodsucker's she-wolf, the one that inflicts death with one bite." His eyes glowed with respect and curiosity. "Why would any of our kind willingly protect a vampire?"

I took one step forward and growled and felt Kane's thought in my head. *Back off, girl. Let's hear them out.* I hesitated, and the pain surged through my brain. *Now. Do as I say.*

I whined and stepped back.

Matteo stood his ground. "We have no quarrel with the first blood son and his pack. All of you defeated our every effort to take territory and business from the Italian vampires."

Zeb scoffed. "They are fearful of your strength, intelligence, and ability to shapeshift, Kane."

"Like my Viking ancestors," Matteo continued, "I will not lose more numbers of my kind in battle.

We ask for a temporary truce with the original vampires and werewolves."

"Temporary?" Kane stroked his chin. "Why temporary? Do you plan more interference with my progeny's business here in Italy? Do you still wish to destroy the vampire line for your own gain?"

Matteo shrugged. "Who is to say what will disrupt our efforts to maintain peace?"

Zachary and Zylon, the terror, stepped to stand with Kane, Zandra, and me. We were soon joined with all the brothers in a line.

"We will not break the peace, but should you do so, you will all die." Kane folded his arms, and his eyes shifted to bloodred.

I stepped forward once more, teeth bared, hackles raised. I sensed half-truths and underlying disagreement in their words. I felt Kane's distrust of them. I thought we would be better off with their deaths. I begged inwardly for one of them to question my master.

Diego surged forward and stood next to his brother. "Why do we have to stand still for this?"

"Shut up, brother!" Matteo barked through clenched teeth.

"It appears you have little in your control, Matteo, even your own brother." Kane smirked, and I moved forward.

Hold off, Moon, unless he makes a move.

"I will not be subjugated to this filthy bloodsucker!" Diego lunged at Kane.

It was the move I had waited for. I leaped, taking down the shifter by his throat and bit into it hard as he screamed.

Diego began to foam at the mouth. All eyes watched him convulse for a brief time.

"Your brother is beyond help."

Matteo, frozen to the spot he stood, stared in disbelief at Diego's dead, open eyes. "This is your version of peace?" Matteo's anger drove him to a partial transformation to wolf. He lifted his morphing snout to the moon and let out a growl that became a howl. The touch of Paolo's hand on his shoulder appeared to steady him, and Matteo forced himself back into his human form.

"If you or your kind seeks out our destruction," Kane waved a hand at Diego, "you will be met with in kind."

Matteo stepped forward and struggled against Paolo's hold as I snarled at him.

"This is what I get for trying to make peace? If you want war, then I will call upon my shifter nation from across the globe." Matteo shoved his brother back to the wall.

"You have a nation of shifters, yes, as do I. And, as you have learned, I have the support of the direct descendants of the originals of your kind. If you don't want more loss, get your packs under control." Kane stepped over Diego's dead body and stood before Matteo, who was visibly shaken along with his remaining brother.

"What is that *thing*?" Matteo pointed to me. "I've heard of her abilities, but this..."

"She is Moon Blood, and she carries a deadly toxin in her bite. That is just one of her many abilities as my progeny. Seek us out if you wish to discover what all of us can do together."

Matteo clenched his fists. I could hear his back teeth grinding. He shot Kane a long, hostile look, and then nodded. He and Paolo lifted their brother and carried him away.

"That was easy." Zandra huffed.

"Too easy." Kane scratched my head and pivoted to the others. "I suspect they will resurface in the future. My guess is that their numbers are depleted, but that they will return when they replenish."

∞

I waited in the foyer of the estate in the alcove under the semicircular staircase listening to a heated discussion among Zandra and her brothers. As soon as Kane left for a meeting with his master vintner in the wine cellar, the descendants of the original werewolf went into a huddle.

"I say we tell him that our packs may not adhere to his agreement with the flesh eaters." Zandra's voice rang with exasperation.

"Not until we know that for certain," Zeb shot back.

Zindel raised his voice to be heard over them. "Our kind has lived in peace with humans and all creatures, but the berserkers can never be trusted. They are greedy and deceptive, and our werewolf nation has tried to live in peace with others but are weary of the exploits of the flesh eaters."

"Wouldn't our good brothers and sisters not want to favor a peaceful truce?" Zoltan's soft voice seemed inappropriate for a man his size.

"That's the point, Zoltan." Zeb spoke with authority. "We won't know until we meet with them. What's the point of adding more worry to Kane's numerous burdens?"

"Because he is so confident that he has everything under control," Zandra urged. "I don't want him to let his guard down. He's weary of battle and wants reprieve, but now is not the time."

Zachary's voice cut through the rumblings of the other brothers. "Let's look at this from a logical point of view. If we meet with our packs over the next week, one of us can return to forewarn Kane if it appears we can't get consensus."

Zandra snapped back. "What do you suggest I tell Kane for our extended absence?"

"Just that we have family business to attend," Zeb offered.

I decided to enter the den at the culmination of their discussion and padded across the wide plank cypress floor covered with a rich tapestry rug that picked up the purple and tans of the room furniture. I plopped down on my plush maroon velvet bed next to the continuous fire that Kane kept ablaze.

Her brothers made a noisy exit through the front door. Zeb yelled over his shoulder, "We'll wait outside for you. Tell Kane whatever you want."

Zandra cocked her head at me, walked over, and knelt next to me. "Moon, I don't know if you heard any of the discussion we just had, but please don't say anything until I return and have time to talk to him." She rubbed my head, and her eyes pleaded with me.

I had no way to answer. Kane only reached into my mind when he sensed fear or anxiety in me. But, because of our connection, he always knew my state of mind. And if Kane asked me point blank if I suspected anything out of the ordinary, I would hold back nothing from him. I looked into her eyes and tried to convey my thoughts with no success.

She sighed and stood just as Kane came striding into the room. He walked to a bar that covered one wall of the room. Crystal bottles filled with brown and red liquid sat on mirrored shelves. Kane filled a pretty wine glass and tossed it down instead of sipping it. Pouring another, he walked to a plush purple velvet chair and sat his glass on the sculpted cypress wooden table that sat between the two identical chairs flanking the fireplace.

Zandra sauntered over to him and sat on the arm of Kane's chair and wrapped her arms around him. "Is everything all right?"

My master sighed. "Yes, just business matters. Nothing serious. But I feel agitated. Can't figure out why."

I understood his concern. I'd felt the same since the redheaded woman and her wolf had approached us.

Zandra took a lock of his long hair and twirled it with her fingers. "I hope this doesn't come at a bad time, but my brothers and I have some family business to attend. We plan to leave early tomorrow during the day. So, we'll be gone when you rise from your rest."

I watched with interest and kept my thoughts to a minimum.

"Oh?" Kane looked up into her eyes. "I'm surprised with your concern for additional attacks that you would want to leave now."

Sidestepping his comment, Zandra slid into his lap and cupped her hands behind his head. "Will you miss me? It's only a week."

Kane's eyes narrowed for an instant, and then he smiled. "Well, I can always entertain the redhead from the festival if I get lonely." He threw back his head and laughed, but Zandra found no humor in his remark.

She jumped from his lap and glared at him. "Really? I thought I meant more to you than that."

He reached up for Zandra's hand, but she snatched it away.

"You are important to me, Zandra. I think we have a great relationship and a reasonable understanding." He stood and towered over her by a head.

"Reasonable understanding? What does that mean?" She glared at her lover.

I jumped up and rubbed myself between them.

Stay out of this, Moon. I think I'm getting into waters I don't want to tread.

"Well, we have fun together. The sex is incredible. We have mutual respect..."

"Is that it? Fun, sex, and respect? What if I want more?" She pulled herself up to her full six feet, hands clenched, jaw jutted in defiance.

"More? What more?" Kane ran his hands through his hair.

"I want the loyalty that I have given to you to be returned in kind." She continued to stare up into his eyes.

"Do you mean you want a monogamous relationship?" Kane clenched his jaw.

"Why not? Is that too much to ask?" The she-werewolf stood her ground.

"That's not something I've ever offered to any woman."

"Wolves mate for life. That's where I'm headed with you. I've put my life and those of my brothers on the line for you more than once. I wouldn't do so if I didn't love you, Kane. If you can't go there with me, it would be best to tell me sooner than later." She swirled and headed for the door. "I'll need an answer when I return." She slipped through the door as Kane, mouth agape, stared after her.

EPiSODE THREE

ATTEMPTED SEDUCTiON

Kane stood in silence for several moments contemplating Zandra's ultimatum and abrupt departure. He reached the bar in two strides, filled a glass with wine, and chugged it.

His action surprised me as he was forever discussing the value of savoring wine.

He swung around to me and thought, *What the hell has gotten into that woman?*

I snorted and sat back on my haunches. *Did you not hear her tell you that she loves you?*

Well, I love her for her loyalty and help through our battles, but that doesn't mean I want to be committed to one woman. Life is too full of delightful females.

I sneezed at that one. *I know one woman that you would commit to if you could.*

He dashed the glass he held into the fireplace, and it shattered and left shards of crystal on the hearth. *How many times must I swear that is never*

*going to happen. My loyalty is to Brogio. It is in my
best interest for him to be happy with Selene.*

James appeared with a broom and dust pan
and swept the broken debris away. As he turned to
go, Kane called out to him. "James?"

The quiet servant halted and head bowed.
"Yes, Master?"

"What do you know of women?"

"Nothing, Master."

"Did you not have a woman before you joined
Brogio's service?"

"I was 18, sir. My only desire has been to
become kindred since I was 12. It is my hope that
my devotion to you as your servant will grant me
that privilege someday." The man scurried away
before he could be questioned further.

James spoke the truth. I had observed him for
years now. He talked only when questioned. He
remained ever vigilant whenever Kane rested, and
he took up weapons and became a fierce warrior in
battles past.

Kane sighed and eyeballed me. *The night is
young. Let's drive into the Taste of Rome and enjoy
the evening.*

*Do you mean the outdoor bar in the medieval
village where we first met Zandra?*

Yes. Barberino Val d'Elsa.

Why do we go there instead of other places?

Kane laughed. *You know me well, my girl. I love its history. I'm drawn to knowledge.*

Remind me of why this place interests you.

The main street connects the two gate towers, Porta Romana and Porta Fiorentina. The history of Barberino is closely tied to the once powerful city of Semifonte, a nearby town destroyed by the Florentines in 1202.

I found history boring but wanted to humor him. *Why is that of interest to you?*

Kane smiled at my question. *It was once a large, important city and considered a great enemy by Florence, just 30 kilometers away. A power struggle allowed Florentines to eliminate the threat. In a four-year siege, it was conquered.*

I scratched an itchy ear. *What happened to the town after that?*

My sire smiled again. *Afterward, Florence prohibited anyone from building there for all time. I love its history and the ancient walls surrounding it.*

Kane drove his Alpha Romeo coupe with the top down, and I stuck my face into the wind savoring the night air filled with the smell of deer, boar, hare, the remains of rotting dead creatures, and wine vines. I never tired of car rides where I could stand in the passenger seat, chin resting on the top of the windshield frame, and breathe in the night and all that it held.

As the last time we visited the Taste of Rome, I sat on the outside of the patio of the ivy-covered old building next to Kane's small table as he enjoyed a glass of Chianti.

I sensed Samil before he arrived to sit next to me. I growled at the black wolf's close presence. Lilith soon entered the patio, glanced around, and flashed Kane a smile that revealed white teeth outlined by dark-red lipstick.

He stood as she approached, and the men at the surrounding tables gawked as she glided over to my sire. The envious stares of the women followed her every movement.

"Lilith, what a pleasant surprise." Kane pulled out a chair for the woman who sent shivers up my spine.

Samil leaped up, barked, and tried to entice me to come and play.

I ignored him, but he persisted.

He nudged my shoulder, backed up, and took a downward dog position with his butt in the air.

I ignored him until Kane looked at me. *Let's play this out and see what they are up to. Follow him wherever he leads.* He returned to Lilith, seemingly enthralled by her. "May I offer you a glass of Chianti? It's quite good here."

No. I will stay by your side.

Disobedient mutt, surged through my brain.

Samil continued to engage me in play. He nipped at my shoulder and then ran off. Getting no reaction, he ran back and butted me with his head.

I growled which only appeared to encourage him.

He sat so close that I had to move over to keep him from sitting on me.

He kept this activity up as I continued to ignore him and snap at him whenever he would nip at me. Intent with the conversation between Lilith and Kane, I stood my ground.

"Where is your lovely girlfriend?" Lilith leaned toward my sire and smiled again.

"With her family." Kane called the waitress over to order his companion wine.

Lilith leaned forward seductively. "I'm sorry to have missed her but lucky to get you to myself."

"Are you truly sorry?"

"Not really."

"Didn't think so."

I didn't like the direction of this conversation.

"What brings you here, Lilith?" Kane took the wine from the waitress and handed it to the woman.

"You do, Kane." She took the wine and sipped it. "Delicious. Both you and the wine." She peered at him over the glass.

"What business do you have with me then?" Kane sat down his glass and held her gaze.

"Business? Who said anything about business?" Lilith leaned forward as the green cowl-neck sweater she wore over a black leather skirt fell off one shoulder. The sweater matched her eyes.

"Then, why were you in Lucca and now here in Barberino?"

"It's simple. As I told you, I'm here for you." She reached across the table and took his hand, squeezed it, and laughed. "I'm with Wines and Vines of the Italian Trade Commission. I wanted to tease you a bit. Word has spread of the handsome owner of the famous Villa Chiantigiana Winery who happens to be a bachelor."

"You live in Los Angeles, then?" Kane withdrew his hand.

"Oh, I live wherever my business takes me." She pulled out a business card and slid it across the table at Kane. "I want to discuss the possibility of your being one of the hosts for a fam trip of Italian wineries for worldwide wine-store owners."

"Ah, I see."

I knew that Kane feigned the acceptance of her presence. He shot me a message. *Let's take this to the next level and see if she reveals her true reason for being here. Play along with me, Moon.*

My master glanced at his Breitling Swiss-made custom watch. "In that case, come to my home for dinner tomorrow night, say eight o'clock? I would stay to discuss this at length, but I have another commitment tonight."

No! I warned. *Don't invite her to our home. She is lying. I don't think she is human. She has an odd smell about her, like fireplace ashes. She appears to float instead of walk. She means you harm.* I whined to emphasize my point, and Samil moved in to lick my face. I growled at him. He ignored me and wet my snout with his tongue. I moved away, but he followed and pressed close to me.

Kane's silent laughter rang in my head. *Well, she isn't after my soul, that's for sure.*

"Why, I'd love to come. A tour of the winery is absolutely in order. But wouldn't it be better seen in the daylight?" She smirked as if she carried an unrevealed secret.

Kane sat back and dismissed her taunt with a wave of his hand. "It would, but I'm completely booked during the day tomorrow... if you don't want to tour at night, perhaps, in say, a week or two?"

"No, tomorrow night will be just fine."

I tried again to stop him from meeting her. *But what about Zandra? You don't act like yourself when you are around Lilith. You are being naïve of the danger she poses.*

Why must you bring up Zandra when all I'm doing is trying to discover what Lilith is up to? Stop worrying so much. Do you really think I can't handle myself?

Kane gave her a broad smile. "Good, I'm looking forward to having you for dinner."

"Likewise," she whispered as she rose from the table.

Samil joined her outside the patio as she snapped her fingers, and they disappeared down the cobblestone street.

∞

My hackles rose as I felt them approaching. I sat on my bed next to the fireplace and waited as Kane opened the door to the visitors I considered threats.

Samil trotted in ahead of his mistress and made a beeline for me. I could only surmise that his purpose was to distract and befuddle me so that I wouldn't pay attention to Lilith. But her attire, or lack of it, made it difficult not to focus on her.

She stood in the doorway, hands on hips, and let Kane take her in. Clad in a sheer emerald-green top that revealed a lacey matching bra and a short, green leather skirt, and stilettos, Lilith left little to the imagination where her body was concerned.

"Come in, Lilith." He glanced at her shoes. "I'm afraid your high heels might not be the most practical for a tour of the winery." He smirked as he closed the door.

"It's of no concern, Kane. I'm quite accustomed to them." She sauntered into the room and gazed at the luxurious trappings of our home. "Quite a lovely home," she muttered. She spun around and put her arm through my sire's and flashed him another ridiculous smile. When she eyed me, her smile widened and showed all her front teeth.

Her aggressive smile is a warning to me.

Kane didn't respond to me. "Thank you. May I offer you a glass of wine? Come sit by the fire. Looks like you forgot your coat on this brisk evening." My sire motioned to a chair, but she ignored him and followed him to the bar.

She appeared intent on forcing her charms on him as did Samil on me. He nipped at me and gave me a playful downward-dog-butt-in-the-air play signal. When I didn't join his invitation to play, he stepped up and stared into my eyes. I felt his seductive draw. His handsome demeanor wasn't lost on me, but I dismissed it to remain vigil for my master.

Samil suddenly leaped up and rushed the front door and filled the air with howls and growls.

Imagine my surprise when a strange voice, *his voice*, slid through my mind. *Danger! Threats! Forest! Now!*

I reacted in an instant. Flesh eaters. I glanced at Kane, who appeared oblivious to anything but Lilith. I rushed the door, too. I leaped up and pulled the door handle down. Samil swung it open with his large snout. We raced to the forest.

Shadowy creatures lurked behind the cedar and oak trees. I couldn't distinguish them. Forms changed shape as I approached. They merged together. A group sprinted through shrubs, trees, over stumps and fallen branches. Prey scattered in terror as I followed.

One form faced me. Its red eyes glowed. I pounced, but it vanished in thin air.

Samil crashed after them. He pounced. They disappeared. Acrid smells filled the air. He lifted his nose and sniffed.

I sneezed as the offensive smell assaulted my snout.

Howls wafted through the air, and we were off again. We continued to chase indistinguishable creatures that evaporated into the air.

After what seemed a long span of time, I skidded to a stop as Samil continued to make chase. We had traveled to the far end of Kane's estate. I shook my head to clear my befuddled mind and connected to Kane. What I saw frightened me.

Lilith had disappeared, and in her place, I saw what Kane did. Selene, beautiful Selene. Clothed in a silver dress, she wrapped her lovely white arms around him and cooed, "But don't you see, Kane. It's you I want, not Brogio. Since becoming human, he is boring. I need excitement. I *need you*. You know you want me... so take me."

Selene moved closer and flashed the same sparkling smile that Lilith used.

I felt my sire back away from her, struggling not to betray his maker. But I could feel the magical, irresistible spell that pulled on him. Like the sirens Kane had described in his mythological stores, this image was the most desirable, the most beautiful woman in the world. Magic made him want her above anyone or anything else. Yet, he backed away further, even knowing that she offered herself to him. I felt his internal struggle to remain ever loyal to Brogio. As he resisted, the fair woman darkened with olive skin, golden eyes, and brown hair.

I felt my master's struggle, but couldn't connect to him. Something blocked me. Lilith had to be preventing me. She controlled Kane's mind.

I swirled around in frustration. I took off on a dead run toward home and concentrated on James. I had never tried as hard to connect with a human before. My feet carried me like lightning, but Samil had distracted me for miles, and I didn't know how much time I had to get to Kane. Stopping briefly, I focused all my energy on James, and then it happened.

James' voice, like a wisp of air, floated through my head. *I am here, Moon.*

Without hesitation, I screamed back to him, *Help Master. He is in danger from the woman there for dinner.*

Only moments later, I connected to Kane and knew that our interlocking minds gave him the extra push to shake off the spell Lilith had cast on him. I arrived in time to witness his smooth handling of the situation.

James stood next to our master, and a perplexed Lilith stood in front of them. Kane was seething inside, but outwardly made his excuses. "I'm so sorry, Lilith, but James has just informed me of some urgent business that can't wait. I'll need to reschedule our tour of the winery and dinner. Perhaps upon Zandra's return next week?"

"Really?" Lilith placed her hands on her hips and thrust her ample chest at both men. "You work at night as well?"

Kane smiled. "My business is conducted throughout the world, Lilith, as you have claimed yours is as well. I'm sure you understand."

"But, my business might not allow me to meet with you next week. Can't you at least spare me another hour?" She walked toward Kane, but James blocked her, gripped her arm, and escorted her to the door. She looked up at him as if to try and place a spell on him. James paused for a moment and struggled to avert his eyes from her and pushed her forward.

Samil entered the door behind me and whined.

Lilith gave him a scathing look, twisted her arm from James' grip, pointed to the door, and threw back over her shoulder, "I'll be back for you, Kane."

I padded over to my master and shot him a message. *That was a close call.*

He walked to a chair near the fire and slumped into it. *What exactly happened? All I remember is you and the wolf bolting out the door after they arrived.*

I sat next to him and stared into his dark eyes. *The wolf distracted me with a ruse, and the woman put a magical spell on you. She appeared as Selene and offered herself to you. When that didn't work, she transformed into Zandra.*

"What the hell!" he yelled aloud.

James walked to the bar and poured his master a tall glass of bourbon, which Kane eagerly took and tossed down his throat.

This is the second time that she's made you think she is Selene. And you appeared spellbound by her. I nudged his hand, and he scratched my head absentmindedly.

I'll admit that Selene was my first love, but I would betray my very existence by ever acting on it. As I confessed to Brogio, I have put it behind me.

We sat together for several moments, and then, dawning realization spread across his face.

Wait a minute. He sprang from his chair and rushed into the library, calling over his shoulder to James and me, "I think I know what's going on here. The two of you wait there."

James tidied up the den, while I stretched out in front of the fire. I closed my eyes and waited, wondering what he might suspect.

What seemed like enough time to hunt and take down prey passed until Kane strode back into the room. "The two of you are not going to believe what I've just verified."

EPISODE FOUR

LILITH

Embarrassment. Kane's embarrassment flooded through my brain.

"I should have picked up on this sooner. Lilith's strength and ability to cast a spell over men is unparalleled. I have no other excuse for missing all the clues—my so-called nightmare, her appearing as Selene, the wolf, Samil."

What do you mean about Samil? But she had no power to disarm James. My mind raced with questions at his comments.

Patience, Moon. I'll reveal all. As for James, his devotion to me supersedes all other emotion. Binding himself as my servant to gain eventual immortality blocks all others from influencing him. He can only become kindred through that loyalty.

Turning to James, he pointed to the chair opposite him. "Gather around you two. I have quite a tale to share.

He marched to the bar, poured two glasses of wine, and handed one to James, who took it with some hesitation.

"Drink up, James. You'll need it to take all of this in." Kane glanced at me. *James is going to be a boring vampire if he doesn't loosen up.*

I padded to my bed next to the fire and sat staring at my sire. I struggled to contain my eagerness to hear what he had to share.

Kane sipped his wine, stretching out my anticipation as he liked to do. He set down the glass and finally began revealing his discovery. "Lilith or Lilit as translated in Hebrew-language texts means 'night creature' or 'night monster.' She is an ancient immortal." He paused to let his words sink in.

Another immortal means us harm?

He ignored my question and continued. "Lilith is often envisioned as a dangerous demon of the night, who is sexually wanton and who steals babies in the darkness."

That must be why the babies and children screamed when she appeared at the festival where we met her.

Yes, Moon, indeed it does seem so.

Kane paused and took another sip of wine. "But it goes much deeper. In Jewish folklore, Lilith appeared as Adam's first wife. The lore in the satirical book *Alphabet of Sirach* showed her being created at the same time of Rosh Hashanah and from the same dirt as Adam. This..."

What is Rosh Hashanah? I blurted into his mind.

It's the beginning of the New Year for those of Jewish descent. He smiled at me and went on. "This contrasted, of course, with Genesis in the Bible where Eve was created from Adam's ribs. Anyway, the legend, which was developed extensively during the Middle Ages, described that Lilith left Adam after she refused to become subservient to him sexually."

James shifted in his chair revealing his discomfort at the mention of sex and nervously sipped his wine.

I urged my master to go on. *What happened to her after she left Adam?*

"She refused to return to the Garden of Eden after she coupled with the archangel Samael, which in Hebrew means 'Venom of God' or 'Poison of God.' But, it's important to know that Samael or *Samil*, is an important archangel in Talmudic and post-Talmudic lore. He is a figure who is an accuser, seducer, and destroyer, and is regarded as both good and evil."

I jumped up at his words. *I saw both good and evil in Samil the wolf's green eyes.*

Makes sense. "But conflicting views say that Samil is actually Satan. Versions of this legend say that Lilith had a sexual relationship with Satan."

So, Samil the wolf is Satan? I chased my tail in my bed to calm my nerves.

"James, Moon just asked if the wolf with Lilith is Satan. I'd gander a guess and say it's a real possibility."

James shook his head, drained his glass, and rose to replenish the liquid for his master and himself.

Kane took the offered glass, took a long pull from it, set the glass down, and began to pace. "After Lilith left Adam, God the Father sent three angels after her and commanded them to bring her back to her husband by force if she refused to go willingly. When the angels found her by the Red Sea, they couldn't force her to obey them, but she struck a strange deal with them." He stopped, picked up his glass, drained the rest of his wine, and plopped back down in his chair.

What kind of deal?

"She promised not to harm newborn children if they were protected by an amulet with the names of the three angels written on it. Then, through her couplings with the devil, or with Adam as his succubus..."

Wait. What's a succubus?

"Moon wants to know what a succubus is," Kane repeated to James. "It's a demon who appears in dreams and takes the form of a woman to seduce men through sexual activity. But let me finish my thought, Moon... through her couplings with the devil, Lilith gave birth to one hundred demonic children a day. In this way, Lilith was held responsible for populating the world with evil."

I stood and shook the chills that ran through my body at Kane's words.

James rose, took both their glasses, and refilled them. "But she didn't create vampires, did she?"

I had never seen James quite so unnerved.

Kane sighed. "No, that handy work was accomplished by Apollo, Artemis, and Hades."

"The mythological gods who plagued your sire made him a vampire?" James' eyes widened as he carried the wine back to Kane.

"Yes. I am surprised you've never heard the story since you worked for Brogio much longer than you have for me." Kane waved his hand in the air as if to dismiss the topic. "But let me stay on point about Lilith." Kane took the glass, placed it next to him, and ran his fingers across his strong brow. "Later legends also characterize Lilith as a beautiful woman who seduces men or copulates with them in their sleep. See the connection? She's a succubus and has been called the first one. She then spawns demon children."

What would happen to you if she had been successful in mating with you?

Kane sighed. "James, Moon wants…"

James' quiet voice interrupted Kane. It was a first. "I know, **Master**. I can now hear Moon's thoughts."

"What? How?"

"She broke through to me to interrupt that *thing* from completing its purpose with you." James sunk into his chair. "Apologies for interrupting you."

"No, James, that's wonderful news!" He looked at me and grinned. "It will save me translation time and serve us well in times of distress." He stood, walked to me, and scratched my head. "Good work, Moon."

I gave him my best smile by panting with my mouth open and my tongue hanging out.

Kane took a sip of wine and continued. "To answer your question, Moon, religious traditions hold that repeated sexual activity with a succubus may result in the deterioration of health or mental state, and even death."

But Lilith has appeared to you in both a dream and in reality. You said her kind appeared in dreams. I padded to him and licked his hand.

"Modern representations say a succubus may or may not appear in dreams. She is depicted as an enchantress where in the past succubi were described as frightening and demonic. She has been called the Queen of demons. Therefore, like all originals, I would expect her to be able to make her presence known in both dreams and reality."

But what is her purpose in mating with men? Is it to produce more demons?

"Moon is perceptive, James. According to the *Witches' Hammer*, written by Heinrich Kramer in 1486, succubi collect semen from the men they seduce. Incubi, or male demons that are the counterpart of succubi, then use the semen to impregnate human females by attacking them at night. This explains how demons can apparently sire children despite the traditional belief that they are incapable of reproduction."

"Good grief," James mumbled and put his head in his hands.

"The children so begotten are called cambions, and many were born deformed or more susceptible to supernatural influences." Kane stretched out his legs in front of him.

James spoke again to my surprise. It must have been the wine that loosened his tongue. "Does this book explain why a human female impregnated with the semen of a human male would not produce regular human offspring?"

"Not really," Kane responded. "But an explanation could be that the semen is altered before being transferred to the female host. In some lore, the child was born deformed because the conception was unnatural."

So, the succubi and incubi work together to produce offspring or demons? I leaned into my master's knee and searched his focused face.

"Some scholars suggest a deeper connection and that the succubi and incubi are, in fact, the same creature and shift between female and male forms, according to their sexual partners." Kane rubbed my head as he spoke.

Lilith must have super powers to be able to put you under her spell. I licked his hand.

"According to my research, Lilith possesses super speed, can materialize and dematerialize in an instant, has super strength, can fly, can suck the life force out of her victims with a kiss, can tirelessly make love and grows stronger as a result, heals from most wounds, makes males crave instant sex, and is immortal." He sighed. "Apparently she can change her shape to match an individual's view of beauty, including becoming the one the male most desires."

That's why she appears as Selene to you.

Yes, Moon, can we get off that for now?

"Well, sir, this explains her presence, doesn't it?" James spoke as he stared at the floor, not daring to meet his master's eyes.

But, you told me long ago that vampires can't procreate by sex. So, why does she want your seed, Kane?

Kane snorted at my question. "Yes, vampires do not procreate sexually, but perhaps since the seed is taken by the incubus it is somehow changed. Regardless, she has singled me out for some evil purpose, and we must destroy her."

EPISODE FIVE

ZANDRA RETURNS

James planted himself against our resting room wall each day to guard against Lilith's intrusion. How the man could go without sleep for days on end mystified me. He watched over us all day and then served Kane's every whim at night. His desire to gain immortality from Kane must have served to enhance his staying power.

All remained quiet until the third day after the she-demon's real-time attempt at overcoming Kane.

My master's thrashing startled me. I awoke out of my rest, growling and partially transforming into my inner demon, a trait I inherited from Kane. With my claws extended and fangs lowered, I attempted to leap onto my sire's chest only to get knocked away by an invisible force. James struggled and forced himself between Kane and the attacker. He managed to push it off our master. Kane, still asleep, continued to fight off the monster inside his nightmare. A force held all three of us from moving at normal speed. I waded like a dreamer trying to push through heavy mud.

The faint outline of a naked she-demon with fangs, claws, bat-like wings, and a long tail that whipped wildly through the air appeared and disappeared at brief intervals. Before I could bury my deadly fangs into her, James put a parrying dagger through her heart.

Kane awoke and bolted upright. He knocked James to the floor and grabbed the visible outline of the now-weakened creature by the throat. His red eyes glowed as he sunk his extended fangs into her jugular. Her high-pitched scream pierced through my sensitive ears, and I snapped at the air in pain as I fell back on the bed once the creature's hold released me.

All three of us, now wideawake, scrambled up and crouched around the large four-poster bed.

I listened for any sign of the demon's presence but sensed nothing.

"She's gone." Kane slumped back on the bed and rubbed his eyes. "Great work, James. I've always wondered why you like to use that parrying dagger, but it appears quite effective. Thanks."

Kane patted the spot next to him, and I used all my waning strength to leap into his lap and cover his face with my wet tongue. He laughed and fell back on the bed with me in his arms. We lay there together in a stupor.

"Why do you think she allowed us to see her, Master?" James leaned back against the wall.

"Perhaps trying to hold the three of us at bay sapped a little of her energy. I'm not sure, but it's fortunate that we were able to do so." Kane rubbed my head, released me, and sat up. The emerging nightfall began to return our strength.

Did she present herself to you again as Selene? I yawned and reveled as I sensed the sun disappear below the horizon.

Kane hesitated for a moment, and then shook his head. "No, she came to me as Zandra. Clever minx that she is... she will attempt to confuse me and get her way."

How did you know it wasn't Zandra? I scratched an ear and settled next to him.

"Zandra said she'd be gone a week. She's smart enough not to try and jump my bones while I am taking my rest from the daylight. Even my subconscious mind knew it couldn't be her."

James leaned forward. "I believe we have not seen the last of her, Master."

"No, James, we haven't, but we'll just have to keep trying to stave her off until I can figure out how to destroy her. I'll spend the night hunting for answers. Perhaps you can prepare some human blood for us to alleviate the need to hunt tonight? Use O Neg for Moon, and I'll try the AB Neg."

We were fortunate that Kane's wealth allowed for him to maintain large stores of black-market human blood for us.

James moved to the door. "Yes, right away, sir." He slipped through the door.

I licked my chops at the thought of such a gourmet meal.

∞

I had just cleaned my bowl when I heard Zandra's voice at the front door.

"Hello, anybody home?"

Kane slammed down his glass and rushed into the den. I followed and stopped at the sight of our she-werewolf friend standing in front of Kane.

She reached out to him, and my master stepped back and sniffed the air.

I joined them and sniffed a whiff of her.

"What in the world are you doing?" Zandra crossed her arms and flashed him an inquisitive frown. "You act like you don't trust me."

"Why would you say that?" Kane eyed her suspiciously.

"Well, why else would you try and scent me out?" Zandra lifted her chin in defiance.

"Zandra, you'll need to just take my word on this. You need to prove to me that you are who you say you are." He circled around her, and she turned to follow his movement as he did so.

"How do I prove it?"

"Answer some questions."

She eyed Kane and gave a nod.

"Where did we meet?"

"The Taste of Rome."

"What did we drink?"

"Wine."

"What kind of wine."

"Your wine."

"What happened at the abandoned winery near Aprigliano?"

"You defeated the berserkers."

"How?"

"You put wolfsbane in their wine. You tricked them like in the Trojan Horse legend."

"What happened to you while you were there?"

"I was held hostage. They slit my throat and put a dagger in my heart. But my brother Zeb removed the knife from my heart, and you healed my throat with your blood."

"Why was it important for Zeb to remove the dagger from your heart?"

"Because I could only live if it was removed by someone who truly loved me." Zandra's eyes narrowed to slits. "I am an original werewolf, and we have the ability to heal beyond what any others of our kind can."

I stepped forward. *How do we know that Lilith doesn't know these things?*

We don't for sure, but she'd have to know an awful lot of detail, plus Lilith hasn't tried to possess her... how could she know? Look how pissed she's getting at me.

Kane stepped forward and attempted to hug Zandra. "Welcome back."

She shrugged off his attempt and marched to the fireplace.

"You're back early." Kane sauntered over to the fireplace and stood next to her.

"That's because I have bad news."

My sire sighed and slumped into a chair next to the fireplace. "What now?"

Zandra sat opposite him and leaned forward. "My brothers and I went to extract an agreement from leaders of my various packs. Several thousand members exist under my command throughout Italy. I had twenty leaders with about one hundred original descendants in each pack."

Kane sat back at the surprising news.

"We went to assure that they would comply with the agreement you made with the berserkers."

"Why am I just learning of this?" Kane leaned toward her.

"I protect my people. My brothers and I have always been capable of supporting your efforts to overcome the berserkers' attacks on you. I didn't want them involved."

Curious as always, I padded over to sit next to Kane. Concern for the bad news to come pressed in on me.

"So, what's the bad news?" Kane rubbed his forehead.

"While we were assembled, a group of flesh eaters led by Matteo Ricci and his remaining brother, Paolo, attacked us in retribution for fighting against them to protect you." She put her elbows on her knees and placed her face in her hands. "It was a bloodbath. We had only assembled the twenty leaders, so it was my brothers and I with them against several hundred."

"Good gods, Zandra, are your brothers all right?"

"Yes, but I've lost five great pack leaders and true friends." A tear round down her cheek.

"I am so sorry for putting you through the interrogation when you arrived. I didn't know." Kane stood and placed a hand on her shoulder.

"What was that all about any way?"

While Kane filled Zandra in on the events while she was gone, I padded into the kitchen and looked for James. He had just finished making the kitchen spotless when he glanced at me.

Come with me. More bad news. Zandra's people have been attacked by berserkers.

The servant followed me and leaned inconspicuously against a wall in the den.

We entered to witness Zandra's jealous reaction to what she'd been told.

"So, in my absence, you invited this strange creature, whom you ran into at the festival and then again at the bar, to your home. Are you mad? Why would you do such a thing?"

Kane smiled. "She said she represented the International Trade Commission and wanted me to host a fam trip for wine owners."

"And, you believed that?"

"No, but Moon and I wanted to find out what she was really up to."

Leave me out of this. I didn't want her coming here.

Shut up, Moon.

"Well!" Zandra marched to the bar and poured herself a glass of brown liquid, downed it, and then spun to stare at her lover with golden eyes that could have shot flames if she had the capability. "I guess you found out that she wanted to have sex with you."

"Look, with Moon's and James' help, we've been able to hold her at bay. She's a demon, a succubus, the *original* succubus. I'll fill in all the details later, but I need to find a way to destroy her." He walked over and put out his hand to her.

She stared at the extended hand and shuffled away. His hand dangled in the air until finally he lowered his arm.

"First, we have a bigger problem as far as I'm concerned. While the group of us were able to destroy our attackers, my packs are on the war path. Matteo escaped with his brother Paolo, but I know they will be back with more flesh eaters. They've made their intent clear. There will be no peace between my werewolves and the berserkers."

So much for their false attempt at feigning peace. I interjected to Kane.

They can never be trusted. My master glanced at me.

"Then Lilith can wait," Kane announced. "You and your people come first."

∞

I became restless. While Kane and Zandra talked, something in the forest pulled at me. I knew that I should stay to be a part of the conversation, but I could think of nothing else but what awaited me in the woods. *I need to patrol the estate, Master. Without Zandra's brothers, it is the needful thing.*

Kane's attention focused on Zandra and the need to resolve the problem we all faced. His command slid back through my mind. *Be careful. Call me if you spot anything.*

I scurried to the door, slapped the latch with my paw, nosed it opened, and ran like the wind to the source that called to me. Scattering squirrels and birds and ignoring delectable prey, I skidded to a stop in front of him.

His green eyes met mine. *Why do you and your master resist us? We will win in the end.*

I stood tall and defiant. *We have overcome worse than the two of you.*

Samil pawed the ground that showed signs of spring. Small green buds forced their way up through the forest bed. *You fascinate me, Moon. Do I not intrigue you?*

I only see you as a threat to my sire.

He took a step and stretched to lick my face, and I backed away. *No closer or I will give you the kiss of death.*

Samil's eyes momentarily glowed and flashed red before returning to emerald. *We know of your deadly bite, but your venom will have no effect on either Lilith or me. We are immortals.*

What do you want of me? Why did you draw me here? I crouched, ready for anything.

I do not want to fight you, Moon. I want you to join me... to be my mate. We can...

NEVER! I scooted backward putting distance between us. *Your intent is evil...* But I sensed something good within him.

Samil shook his head and bared his teeth, but not at me. He appeared to struggle inwardly. *She will overcome your master, Moon. She always does. And when it happens, she will make him her possession. She will control the most powerful vampire in existence... the first blood son of the original. Their evil will consume the world.*

I shivered at his words.

He took a step forward. *Yield to me now and come under my protection.*

My loyalty lies with Kane. If he perishes, then so will I.

I won't let her destroy you. You will belong to me.

My hackles rose. *And spread evil throughout the world? I think not. If you wish to populate the Earth with hybrid demons, know that vampires cannot have offspring.*

Samil's eyes glowed again and changed to red. *Don't be foolish. With me you can procreate.*

I do not wish to be your mate.

Then, why did you come to me when I called you? He took a step forward, and his eyes glowed green again.

You know that you pulled me here. I come to protect Kane. I backed up and bared my teeth, my growl rumbling from my chest.

Moon, I don't want to destroy you, but I will.

I whirled once and used all my preternatural strength to leap at him. I hit the ground just as he vaporized into thin air. Shaking off the grip he'd had on me, I circled around to see if he might be hiding among the trees. I sniffed the air and scented only a faint acrid smell that dissipated. Turning, I scouted the entire perimeter of the estate. Finding nothing, I ran home to Kane.

∞

I slipped through the door, and Kane's eyes questioned me. *Samil lured you to the forest?*

Yes, Lilith and Samil want to control us to spread evil. I attacked, but he disappeared into thin air. I padded over to Kane and licked his hand. He rubbed my head and then joined Zandra who stood in front of the fire warming her backside.

"Lilith and Samil are still lingering around. Moon just saw the succubus' demon wolf in the forest. I suspect the wolf is merely a body that Satan has possessed." He rubbed his chin.

She gave him a weak smile. "It's hard to know which evil to tackle first at this point."

"No." Kane took her hand, and she finally let him. "It's not. It's early. How far away are your pack leaders and brothers?"

"Two hours by the car that I drove." Zandra squeezed his hand and dropped it.

"Then, we'll travel on foot. It'll be faster. I'll carry you since you won't be able to keep up."

"What?" Zandra protested.

"Trust me and hold on." Kane picked up Zandra and headed to the door.

James was already opening it for him. The man had to be psychically connected to our master.

You're with me, Moon. Our speed. He went out the door and became almost invisible as he traveled so fast.

I caught up to his heels and tracked him. We covered the distance in the time it usually takes me to sprint Kane's entire property.

We found the brothers and pack leaders in a small encampment outside the village of Siena. They all were nursing wounds but appeared to be on the mend.

Not knowing us, the pack leaders immediately leaped up and began to transform for battle.

Zeb stilled them by placing his body in front of ours. "This is Kane and his hybrid wolf, Moon. We have fought side by side against the berserkers with them."

"And they're the reason the flesh eaters are out for our blood!" A broad man almost as tall as Zeb faced Zandra's eldest werewolf brother.

"Nardo, calm down." Zeb took a step forward.

Zandra quickly stepped around her brother while Kane stayed back to consider the situation. "Listen to me. I am the eldest original. You have always trusted me. These berserkers' greed for power would have pushed them to attack us even if we had not helped the Italian vampires they sought to destroy. They want to not just control vampire business, but our business."

The remaining pack members gathered behind and beside Nardo.

Kane stepped up next to Zandra. "You have no reason to trust me. We have always been mortal enemies. But I swear on a blood oath to all of you that I will find a way to resolve the endless attacks these warmongers continue to inflict."

Before Nardo could respond, the ground rumbled. All those not standing jumped to their feet. Blurry flashes of fast-moving furry creatures emerged from the surrounding trees.

"Berserkers!" Nardo yelled.

Almost a hundred berserkers swarmed the encampment and began to attack the remaining twenty-eight of us.

The pack leaders, Zandra, and her brothers morphed into werewolf form, slashing at the enemy. Two berserkers tried to grab Zandra from behind, but I leaped on and took down her attackers and tore out their necks. She made quick work of her frontal attacker by ripping off his head.

Kane rushed to yank three off Zeb until he could transform. The other brothers morphed in the blink of an eye and did the same for the pack leaders. Zachary, Zale, and Zander each took on two or three berserkers at a time. Zeno and Zindel, even as they transformed to wolf form, double-teamed ten flesh eaters and ended them. Zylon, who had grown to almost ten feet, lifted three attackers in each arm and smashed their heads together. Zohar somersaulted over the heads of two berserkers and took off their heads as he flipped. Zoltan might be sensitive in everyday life, but he had become a terror on the battlefield, ripping out hearts one after the other. Zane, on the other hand, played with his prey like a cat does with a mouse. He dodged and weaved the enemies' lumbering swipes and then deftly plunged a dagger into their hearts and twisted their heads off as he went.

I skirted through embattled legs, took chunks of flesh as I passed enemies, and rendered numerous berserkers foaming and dying from my deadly bite.

Kane sped from one flesh eater to the next tearing off their heads with lightning speed. As their numbers dwindled, I saw Matteo and Paolo dashing off into the darkness.

I gave chase until Kane's command stopped me.

Let them go for now, Moon. Come back and help finish off the others.

Zandra and her brothers were incredible fighters. They appeared to have ten times the strength of normal werewolves and took on two or three enemies at a time. Zandra, now a full-blown dark-brown wolf, eviscerated several flesh eaters before I could pause to watch. Lithe and acrobatic, she ripped and shredded heads and hearts. The pack leaders, while not as ferocious as their makers, held their own. They each took their enemy counterparts one-on-one and avoided being mortally wounded.

I lowered my body almost to a belly drag and used my vampire speed to swerve through the enemies' legs, biting them as I went. They fell to the ground in mid-fight as I surged through them and my deadly bite ended them.

I came up short when the enemy had been decimated.

The bloody ground was littered with torn arms, legs, hearts, and heads. The clothing of our werewolf friends lay in tatters and was scattered among the bloody scene. Everyone ceased fighting and looked around for more attackers. Finding none, they transformed back into their human form. Bones cracked, spines straightened, limbs and snouts shortened, fur became skin, and our friends stood upright.

Kane tried to wipe the blood from his clothing and face. I sat down and licked my bloody legs. Neither of us had used our abilities to transform into any image we imagined—gifts that we had received when we became kindred. Instead, we found our natural forms more than effective.

Kane sprinted to me, checked me over, and then moved to Zandra, who appeared not to have been injured.

He found a fallen tree limb and perched on it, and I padded over to lick the blood from his hands and face. He wrapped his arms around me and held me close. *Good girl, Moon.*

Zandra joined us on the limb and wiped the blood from her legs and arms.

Kane reached over and brushed the bloody debris from her beautiful face with his shirt sleeve.

My master and I stood as Nardo and the other pack leaders approached. I wasn't sure if they would attack or not.

Nardo held out his hand to Kane, who shook it.

"Thank you for your help. I think we understand now that you are different than we thought you were." Nardo swept his arm to indicate his fellow Lycans agreed with his words.

Then, the pack leader's eyes fell on me. They were filled with admiration and something else. The look he gave me was the same that James gave Kane.

The word is "reverence," Moon. Kane glanced at me and smiled. My sire scratched my head with his fingers. "Moon and I are pleased to help. Your sires have aided us more than we can ever repay." Kane gave Nardo a slight bow.

"Perhaps you can." Nardo's pursed his lips together. "Our flesh-eating counterparts have declared a blood feud and won't stop until they destroy us. Tell us how you can help us end this senseless slaughter."

Kane sighed and ran his still-bloodied hands though his long dark hair. "I don't yet know, but I will soon. I swear it."

EPISODE SIX

THE LYCAN SOLUTION

"Is there no other way?" Zandra sat next to the fireplace the next night, hands clasped in her lap, agitation spreading across her beautiful face.

"I can't think of a cleaner solution." Kane poured her a glass of wine and placed it in her hands.

"Cleaner for whom?" She took a sip of the Chianti and sat it on the side table next to her.

I sat next to Zandra just as dumbfounded as she was at what my sire had just suggested.

Zandra sighed. "Okay, so you want to turn me into a vampire Lycan. What will that enable me to do?"

"Not just you, Zandra, but your brothers as well."

"Why?"

Kane sat opposite her after pouring himself a glass of wine. "All eleven of you are direct descendants of the original werewolf. Like me, as the son of the original vampire, you carry a special gene that gives you far superior abilities than your progeny. Only that gene will allow you to become a hybrid. But being hybrids would allow you to possess the combined powers of both werewolf and vampire, including physically enhanced powers and mind control. You would be more powerful than either species and would grow stronger with age."

I shot a question to my sire. *But you want to give them the mind control that you possess?*

"Moon makes a valid point. The purpose of you and your brothers becoming hybrids is to give you the ability to control both the berserkers and your packs and prevent conflict between them and, hopefully, squelch any desire to make further war with my race." Kane took a sip of wine and sat back in his chair.

"You speak," Zandra leaned forward, "as if you have personal knowledge about hybrids."

Kane sighed. "I do."

"Do other hybrids exist?" Zandra pressed.

"No, not now. Brogio destroyed them long ago."

Why? I interjected.

"They had the ability to match his strength. He couldn't allow those without his wisdom to control the vampire legions." Kane twiddled his glass of wine between his fingers.

Zandra was silent for a moment and then asked, "You think my brothers and I have wisdom enough not to take over your progeny?"

"You've proven it."

Some of the tension Zandra held in her shoulders dissipated. "So, how does that work? How do you turn us?"

"By consuming a large amount of my blood after I've taken you to the point of death. Not just the small amount it took to heal you when you were dying before. I would give my blood to you and each of your brothers."

Concern spread across the she-werewolf's face. "Wouldn't that be dangerous for you? To give up that much of your blood?"

"It's just as dangerous for you."

I licked Zandra's hand. *You and your brothers would be able to hear me, and I wouldn't be the only hybrid in the family.*

Kane laughed. "Moon is excited for you to be able to hear her thoughts."

Zandra scratched my head, smiled, and retreated to deeper contemplation. Finally, she pressed Kane for more details. "How would we be able to control the berserkers?"

"You are the direct descendants of the original. Every other werewolf, except the berserkers, has descended from you and your brothers. Once you are a vampire-Lycan hybrid, you will be able to bring the flesh eaters under your mind control. They won't have the ability to resist you. Once Brogio defeated the slashers that tried to take control of the vampire nation, he controlled the rest of us and taught us to live in the shadows and coexist with humans. As I was his first blood son, he passed that ability to control all others to me. A vampire original Lycan hybrid technically should be able to do the same for the werewolf nation."

Zandra sighed. "That could work. So, besides superhuman strength, what other powers would we possess?"

Kane sipped his wine. "Enhanced superhuman speed. Your speed will surpass that of all others, except mine." His eyes sparkled at her over his wine glass as he took another sip. "Endurance to sustain punches, blows, or wounds while still fighting back. Agility to move, jump, climb, run without difficulty or exhaustion. Keener senses. Stakes and arrows won't stop you, even if they hit you in the heart, but you have that now. Just renders you unconscious until removed by one who *loves* you."

Zandra raised an eyebrow at the emphasis Kane placed on the word *loves*. "So basically, everything we can already do but enhanced. What about other traumas or toxins like silver?"

"That's the beauty of it. There's so much more. You'll heal even faster from trauma than you do now. For instance, if your neck is broken, you'll merely fall unconscious and then heal. You'll be more tolerant and recover more quickly from silver and wolfsbane. Three metals can pierce through immortal skin: imperial gold, celestial bronze, and stygian iron. It burns out whatever it cuts through. So, avoid those. Things like vervaine or wood that normally affect a vampire won't harm you. And you'll be immune to werewolf venom, unlike me." Kane smiled into Zandra's eyes. "Of course, if a silver nitrate grenade is detonated inside you, it might kill you. But hybrids can recover even from death. With one exception."

"Yes, like now, if my head is separated from my body, I will die." Zandra made a cutting movement with her hand across her throat and crossed her eyes. "What else? Will I never see daylight again?"

"On the contrary, you'll still be a day walker. And at night you can attempt to control my dreams or distort my reality. Better watch out though. I might think you're Lilith." He laughed, and she threw a throw pillow from behind her back at him.

"Be prepared to be able to exert control over your emotions as I do. You'll even be able to turn off your humanity."

"Will I still be able to transform into my wolf form at will?" Zandra stood and stretched.

"Yes, and move things with your mind."

"What? You mean I could pick you up and throw you by just thinking about it?" She eyed him and smirked.

"Probably. And like Moon, here, you'll have a sense of things to come." He scratched my neck.

"Do you mean I'll have the gift of foresight?"

Kane nodded his agreement. "And you will be driven as you are now to unite individuals into a whole, like your packs." He stood and faced her, and I moved to my bed next to the fireplace.

Zandra made a clicking sound with her tongue and cheek and crossed her arms. "All that seems well and good, but what are the draw backs?"

Kane touched her cheek and looked into her eyes. "You'll experience emotions more powerfully than humans or regular vampires, especially anger or rage. You'll be prone to violence at first." His eyes twinkled as he spoke. "You will forever feel gratitude and commitment to me, causing you to obey me when I ask you to do so."

"What!" Zandra stamped her foot. "How do I get around that?"

Kane threw back his head and laughed. "Once you've transformed an excess of 100 times in a row, you will break the sire bond."

Are you pulling her leg? I shot to him.

Zandra narrowed her eyes at him. "You're kidding, right?"

Of course, I am. His grin gave his prank away, and she punched him in the arm.

He took her by the shoulders and sat her back down in her chair. As he leaned over her, his brown eyes bore into her gold ones. "Now listen to me carefully. This is important. You must drink human and animal blood or eat animal flesh. As a hybrid, you'll need to feed on blood to remain immortal. Because of the vampire side, hybrids can desiccate without blood or enough meat. It's painful if you don't, even though eating meat will help alleviate the pain. I know your brothers will be glad to learn that."

Zandra took a deep breath. "Will I be dead?"

"As dead as I am. You no longer will need to breathe, but most likely will out of habit."

"Any other zingers about which I need to know?"

Kane cringed. "You won't be able to have children, but your brothers will."

Zandra lifted her chin. "I decided long ago that bringing a child into this life would be cruel. What else?"

Kane turned away from her. He glanced at me with pity in his eyes as he went to refill their wine glasses. Over his shoulder, he muttered, "If you fall in love, that feeling never fades away and is eternal… I think that comes from Brogio and his eternal love of Selene. Only the bond between mates overcomes the competitive drive for blood. If you are romantically bound to someone before you turn, that love will remain for eternity."

I heard Zandra take a sharp breath in, but she said nothing for a moment. "I'll need to speak to my brothers. I'll take the car..."

A knock at the door disrupted her, and I rushed the entryway, growled, and barked. I lifted my nose to the acrid air and knew Lilith stood on the other side. I had been so distracted by Kane's interchange with Zandra that I hadn't sensed her presence before she knocked.

James appeared at my side and placed his hand on my head as if to indicate I should back off. I stood my ground.

"It's all right. Let her in."

I swirled and shot a warning. *NO! She wants to control you.*

Trust me, Moon.

James opened the door, but the smile froze on Lilith's face when she spied Zandra.

I guessed she must have been impervious to the cool night air, as vampires are, because the sheer black lace dress she wore didn't hide her so-called charms.

Zandra moved next to Kane and took his arm. "Well, well. Looks like the wine salesgirl is back to try and persuade you to work with her."

"Vice president of the Italian Wine Commission, dearie. My, you look flush. Lover's quarrel?" Lilith glided in and stood before Zandra and attempted to touch her cheek.

Zandra's upper lip rose showing white teeth, and her inner wolf growled at the woman and threatened Lilith not to touch her.

Kane took Lilith's elbow and started to escort her to the door that James still held open. "What can I do for you, Lilith? Your... uh... unexpected visit has somewhat interrupted a personal conversation."

"Oh, we have unfinished business, don't we, Kane? Why don't I come back later after you finish with your... friend?" Lilith attempted to wrap her arm around Kane's waist, but he deftly removed it, tucked it under his elbow, and mostly dragged her to the door.

"Later, would be inconvenient. I'll call you when I'm free."

The succubus whirled, bringing his arm around her as she leaned up against his chest. "If you don't, I'll be back."

I growled, and in that instant, Zandra slid up to Kane, placed a palm against the middle of Lilith's chest, and shoved the demon out of the house.

James slammed the door after her and stepped back to ready himself for an attack. Surprisingly nothing happened.

Zandra stepped closer to my master. "I don't dare leave tonight."

Kane squeezed her shoulder. "It doesn't matter. She comes to me in dreams, or nightmares, if you will. Last time, she tried to fool me by appearing as you."

They walked back to the fireplace in the den.

"All the more reason for me to be by your side. At least if I'm here, you'll know it's not me, and we can all wake you." Zandra's eyes pleaded with him.

"Zandra, this visit was just a taunt. She appears to be playing with us. And I don't want to put you in harm's way. Surely you know the legend of the succubus and incubus?"

"Yes." Zandra nodded. "Succubus steals the male sperm, and the incubus impregnates an unsuspecting female by raping her."

"Exactly. Let's not make it convenient for her." Kane gingerly wrapped his arms around her, and she hugged him back.

"I'd like to get my hands on some imperial gold, celestial bronze, or stygian iron. That would slow her down."

Kane sighed. "Already thought of it. Unfortunately, she's so ancient that it would do little more than slow her down. Stop worrying about Lilith for now. Your problem is the more pressing in my mind. I have Moon and James. James insists on standing guard in our resting room while we sleep. He'll wake me if he sees unusual movement or me trying to fight an entity off."

The she-werewolf searched his eyes. "Are you sure?"

"Yes, go talk to your brothers and decide if you are all willing to undergo the hybrid transformation. We'll need some time for all of you to acclimate to your new lifestyle." Kane pushed Zandra toward the door.

She kneeled next to me and searched my eyes. "Moon, promise me that you'll not let anything happen to Kane. I'm counting on you."

I barked twice and put my paw on her shoulder.

She hugged me and then was gone.

A chill ran through me. I had no confidence that I would be able to fight off two powerful immortals, especially if Samil was Satan.

∞

As promised, James remained alert while Kane and I rested in our safe room. To our surprise, neither Lilith nor Samil returned while Zandra conferred with her brothers.

Two nights after Zandra had rejoined her siblings, Kane and I entered the house after we finished a run for nightly prey. We had enjoyed the life force of a mountain lion and a dip in a nearby lake. Kane, now dressed in a blue, long-sleeved Tom Ford T-shirt and the same designer's jeans, pulled on his DaVinci black boots just as the front entry door swung open.

Zandra and her ten brothers overwhelmed the entryway. Even the expansive foyer couldn't dwarf the massive frames of these firstborn of the original werewolf.

Kane rose from his chair by the fireplace and waved. "Welcome, Moretti clan. Have you had supper?"

The brothers followed their sister's lead as a determined Zandra marched into the den. She ignored my master's invitation for a meal. "We have discussed your resolution to our problem, Kane." She indicated her siblings by waving back at them.

Zeb stepped up next to his sister. "After lengthy discussions, Zandra has answered all our questions regarding this transformation process."

Zylon leaned against the den wall, his arms crossed in front of his chest. He snorted. "I'm not sure why we need to become hybrids. Are we not powerful enough as direct descendants of the Original?"

Zandra moved toward her battle-scarred brother. "We've been over this. Over our own people... yes. But we can't control an entire nation of berserkers who have defied us since the beginning of their existence. They are a dangerous offshoot of our lineage."

Zylon shrugged as Zachary stepped next to Zandra. "It is the logical way to handle this and preserve our packs. Enough blood has been shed."

Zandra whirled around to the rest of her brothers. "Are we all in agreement, or not?"

All but Zylon shouted, "Yes."

Zandra raised her eyebrows at her terrifying holdout.

"Hmm... yes. It would be worthwhile to be even more powerful in battle if necessary."

"That's not the point, Zylon. Our purpose will be mind control."

I noticed a twinkle in Zylon's eyes as he spoke. "Well, that might be fun as well."

Once the last brother agreed, Zandra faced Kane. "Yes, we are ready to begin. Can we do so now?"

My master smiled. "Do you not wish to feast on meat before we begin? James readied a meal for you in anticipation of your return. After the transformation, your diet will be primarily blood with meat as only a backup."

Zeno headed toward the dining room and threw back over his shoulder, "Then, let's eat."

All but Zandra followed. "I have no need to eat. Transform me now."

Kane placed his hands on his lover's shoulders. "Are you sure?"

"Yes. I don't know how long we'll have until the flesh eaters attack again. Let's not waste time."

"Then, come upstairs. I have a bedroom prepared for each of you." He took her hand and led her up the spiral stairway.

Zandra trotted behind him. "You were that sure of the outcome?"

Kane looked back at her. "You came to me for a solution. I couldn't imagine you would refuse it without another to replace it."

I padded behind them, curious to see how this would work.

Kane took Zandra into the bedroom next to our resting room. I slipped through the entryway and sat in the corner.

"This will be somewhat painful. First, I will drain about half of your blood—"

"Half?" Her voice betrayed nervousness. She was steady in front of her brothers, but this decision cost her.

"Yes. At least." Kane's lips thinned.

"Why didn't I transform into a hybrid when you found me in the Berserkers' stronghold?"

"I didn't perform what Brogio called 'the embrace.' You only had a small taste to heal you." He continued when she still looked confused. "I will take you to the point of death, give you a taste from my wrist, and then infuse my stored blood into you. When the mixture of our blood combines, and you take a large amount of my blood to mingle with yours, it doesn't just heal you. It changes you."

"Then you'll be left weakened." Zandra searched his face with the usual concern she had for my sire.

"That is why I needed to prepare if you agreed to the change."

I had watched James do the bloodletting each of the two previous night so that each of the eleven bedrooms upstairs had transfusion drip bags in a corner of the room. This allowed for Kane to provide an adequate amount of blood directly from him for all of them without incapacitating himself.

"Still, there's only Moon and James while we recover."

"I'll use human blood that I have stored downstairs for a faster recovery. Ready?"

Zandra nodded.

Kane pushed the hair away from her neck, embraced her, and bit into her beautiful olive-skinned neck. The sound of it made me think of James biting into an apple as he often did.

A small squeak erupted from Zandra's parted lips followed by deathly silence.

I padded over to him just as he licked the wound closed on her throat.

He picked the she-werewolf up and gently placed her on the large king-sized bed that appeared identical to the one in our resting room.

Kane then bit into his wrist and placed if over her mouth while dribbling his blood into it. Zandra instinctively began to suck. After a few moments, Kane removed his wrist from her and with some urgency grabbed the blood transfusion stand, bag, and intravenous line from the corner. He carefully inserted the needle on the end of the line into a blood vessel in Zandra's arm, released the clamp that held the blood in the bag, kissed her forehead, and stepped back. *We will let her rest now, Moon, as the virus in my blood grips her. I'll start the process with her brothers and then return. By then, she should be transforming.*

I followed him as he repeated the process with each brother. Several hours later, we returned to Zandra. I am no longer easily shocked, but the sight of Zandra changing back and forth from her werewolf form to the state of something in-between a wolf and a vampire rocked me.

Her body struggled as she screamed and growled. The room filled with the sounds of bones cracking. Her face distorted into a point. Her skin became a motley gray. Fangs dropped and pushed her mouth open. Her eyes flew open and changed from gold to bloodred. Her fingernails and toenails became talons, and she swiped the air with them. She let out a howl and then hissed like a cat.

My hackles rose at the sight of her continuous transformation from wolf to vampire.

Kane stood next to me with his hand on my head. *Stay calm. Let the process finish.*

I could hear the loud screams and howls of Zandra's brothers ring throughout the house. I saw James rush past the bedroom door, seemingly to attend to the siblings who had begun the transformation as well. Several other black-clad servants followed him.

A loud scream pierced my ears, and I jerked my head around to see Zandra rise slightly from the bed, fall back, and transform into the beautiful woman she had always been.

Kane walked to her, removed the needle from her arm, and soothed her forehead with his hand.

She opened her eyes, which were at first coal-black but then dissipated into her usual golden orbs.

Kane helped her sit up. "How do you feel?"

"Exhausted." She jerked her head toward the bedroom door at the sudden howls and screams that assaulted the hallway. "What? Are those my brothers?"

"Yes. Don't be concerned. They are finishing the transformation. Now rest. I am quite depleted and need to refortify with some human blood." He stood and put his fingers over her eyes. "Rest."

I followed him out into the hall and down the stairs and into the kitchen. We both came to an abrupt halt.

Lilith stood with one of the black-clad servants that had been helping James with the brothers' transformation. She bent him over the kitchen counter with her mouth wide and hideous as she sucked his life force from his body. It appeared that she sucked everything from him since the poor man shrank and shriveled up. Lilith released his husk which fell like a piece of clothing to the floor.

Unable to move since Lilith held us at bay, we watched as she ripped open the blood bag James had laid out for his master and emptied the contents into her mouth. She wiped her lips, swung her feral glowing green eyes to us, and smiled. Blood dripped from the corners of her mouth. "Did you think you could be rid of me so easily?"

My master's weariness seeped through my body. I had little confidence that he could fight off her attack. He had just fed his blood to eleven others, and Lilith blocked the source of his strength. Despite my doubts, he focused on his feelings for Zandra and ripped through her blocking veil and jumped on the succubus.

She whirled and gripped him with a force of strength that made me immobile as well.

Kane tried to move as did I, but it felt like wading through heavy mud.

Lilith's laughter permeated throughout the room. She became translucent and bent to his mouth. She opened hers and tried to draw his life force from him.

"You forget, bitch, I have no soul for you to take." He shoved her with all his might, and she hit the refrigerator with such force that the door broke and the room shook.

Lilith lost her grip, and I charged her but hit the refrigerator and almost knocked myself out as she vanished into thin air. I plopped to the floor but jumped up and spun around ready to reattack.

Kane rushed the hanging refrigerator door, yanked it off its remaining hinge, and let it fall to the floor. He grabbed another bag of blood, bit into it, splattering it everywhere, and sucked as much of its contents as possible.

A familiar pull jerked me around, and Kane and I both thought the same name. *Zandra.*

With our vampire speed, we were both up the stairs and burst in on a scene that again stopped us in our tracks. A naked *Kane* stood on his knees between Zandra's legs as he removed her clothing!

"What the hell!" Kane roared.

Lilith tried to create a diversion from this in the kitchen. I growled and bared my fangs.

His counterpart whirled around to face him. Green eyes glowed from the otherwise familiar face.

Kane bounced upon him and yanked the counterfeit off the now-hybrid vampire Lycan, who sat up in confusion. "Kane?" She looked from one to the other.

The imposter flew from Kane's hands and rolled across the floor into the hallway. He began to transform as he rolled and became Samil.

"You will not impregnate her with demon seed!" Kane and I rushed to the wolf who disappeared. We knew he had not yet begun the act since Zandra still remained clothed.

My sire and I bolted down the stairs. We skidded on the marble floor and looked up. A laughing Lilith stood with Samil at the top of the upstairs landing. As we flashed up the stairs, Samil absorbed into Lilith. The combined two rushed into Zandra's bedroom and slammed the door.

Growls and screams emerged within the room.

Kane crashed through the door. We rushed in to see a transformed Zandra wringing Lilith's neck.

Zandra had grown to some ten feet as part wolf and part vampire. Fangs and claws ripped at the succubus who kept appearing then disappearing. Grasping the demon, Zandra broke its neck and bit into her. The succubus/incubus dissolved in her hands.

Bones cracked. Zandra gradually transformed into her human form and plopped down on the bed. She looked at us and smiled. "I have to say that was fun."

Kane couldn't help but laugh. "Yes, being a hybrid has its advantages."

Have we seen the last of her, Master? I looked up at Kane.

Instead of hearing his expected voice, Zandra responded, *She's immortal, Moon. She will just regroup and come back, along with her wolf.*

You can communicate with me telepathically now, Zandra?

It appears so, Moon.

I jumped up and down and barked, and the two of them laughed.

James appeared at the door. "I am sorry, Master. I had my hands full with the brothers." He pointed behind him as the ten of them jockeyed for position behind him, practically knocking him down.

"What did we miss?" Zylon barked.

"Calm down, boys. You're going to love what we've all become." Zandra smiled and winked at Kane.

Kane returned her wink and then faced the brothers. "May I suggest that we all take a run in the woods for some blood prey? You must feed. Then you'll need to take some rest during the daylight hours to let your strength fully mature. So that Moon and I can accompany you, we will begin to bring the berserkers under control tomorrow night."

The brothers were already halfway down the stairs at the mention of prey, and Zandra, Kane, and I brought up the rear.

What if Lilith or Samil returns while we rest? I couldn't stop worrying about what was going to happen next.

Zandra reached out and touched my head as we ran together. *Let them try. I don't need to rest during the day, and I will be next to both of you.*

∞

I'm having second thoughts about how you should approach controlling the berserkers. Kane gathered with Zandra and her ten brothers around the large dining-room table.

I sat next to him as he scratched my ears. Spoken words no longer held worth among us. I found it delightful to be able to communicate with all of them, even James.

Zandra reacted first. *What do you mean? Wasn't our transformation meant to provide us the ability to control our enemies' minds?*

They aren't enemies, Zeb interjected. *They are insignificant insects.*

Kane ignored Zeb's superiority complex and moved on. *The longer I think about it, the more I feel that controlling the minds of just the berserker leaders would take a twenty-four-by-seven effort from each of you, much less trying to keep everyone in line.*

I leaped up, excited by an idea. *What if each of you compelled them to go to sleep?*

What? Zachary leaned toward me. *Do you mean sleep for a century or more?*

Kane stroked his chin. *Hmm… could work.*

I say we do it the old-fashioned way, within the pack mentality accord. Zindel smiled, quite pleased with his suggestion.

Yes! Zylon slammed his fist on the table and startled me.

Why not? Zeno nodded in agreement.

You want to challenge the current pack leader for dominance? Zoltan leaned on his elbows on the table and stared at Zindel.

Zeb spoke before Zindel could respond. *Yes. It is the way. We are stronger than any berserker now. It would only take us challenging Matteo and Paolo to get the European berserker nation to bow to our wishes.*

I padded over to Zeb. *Challenge? Do you mean fight for leadership?*

Zeb patted my head. *Smart girl. Exactly. It is our custom.*

Zandra stood and walked over to her brother's chair. *It won't work. The berserkers have never followed pack norm. They only live to kill and eat flesh. How do we know if we defeat an Alfa the rest will accept one of us as their leader?*

You don't. Kane stood. *It didn't work for me when I fought Agnar at the Ruins of Etrurian Temple of Belvedere in Orvieto. However, I was not one of your kind. Have any of you ever challenged the berserkers for leadership?*

Zohar and Zander both shot a definitive *No* to everyone.

Then, it's really your choice. You said, Kane turned to Zandra, *that you wanted to avoid further bloodshed...*

But, I LIKE bloodshed! Zylon pounded his fist again.

Quiet, brother! Zandra challenged Zylon with her eyes that shifted from gold to red and back. She looked back and responded to Kane's comment. *I do want to avoid bloodshed.*

Zandra's sharp intake of breath made me remember how Kane told her she would no longer need to breathe but would do so out of habit.

But it would only be the loss of two flesh eaters and might multiply our numbers with loyal berserkers. Zandra sat back down and contemplated her own thoughts.

Zeb snorted. *Do we really want those subhuman insects as part of our family?*

We could always try it. Zale, who sat next to his sister, placed his hand on her arm. *If it doesn't work, we could resort to Moon's idea of putting them all to sleep.*

I vote we challenge for leadership. Zylon once again pounded the table.

Zane, who usually remained as quiet as Zander, agreed.

Zylon, I would appreciate it if you wouldn't break my table. I had it made hundreds of years ago and have fond memories around it. Kane stared at the embattled Viking brother.

Zylon reached out with his hands and smoothed the table in front of him. *Sorry.*

Zandra stood. *As the leader of all werewolves, and now of all hybrids, I have decided. We will fight for leadership.*

I am surprised you didn't come to this conclusion before now. Kane raised his eyebrows at Zandra. *You might have avoided the transformation if you had. I shouldn't have assumed you'd already taken that route.*

Zandra rose up to her full six feet and stared into his eyes. *I never considered it because, as mentioned earlier, berserkers have never followed pack accords. They are rebels, terrorists if you will.*

They are subpar creatures who are not worthy of us. We didn't want them to be part of our family. Zeb's lip snarled to match his opinion.

And yet, here you are. Kane turned his head and smiled at Zeb who crossed his arms without further response.

As your leader, Zandra began, *I will be the one to challenge the brothers and fight them.*

A collective *NO* shot through the minds of everyone.

Zeb leaped to his feet almost knocking over the heavy chair in which he had been sitting. *No! I will be the one. You are too important to risk your life with this scum.*

Zandra spun toward her brother, the veins in her neck distended. *I am the oldest, and your leader. I will take consensus only so far. I have fought and killed more enemies than you.*

Kane placed his arm around Zandra in support. *As much as I hate to admit it, Zandra is right. She as your leader should be the one to challenge Matteo and Paolo. This will be a ritual fight, but we will all be there to make sure it stays that way.*

I walked over and stood by Zandra and Kane. My heart felt like a heavy stone.

Zeno, Zane, Zohar, and Zindel grumbled. Zeb sat down and put his head in his hands. Zachary declared it the logical thing to do. Zoltan, Zander, and Zale took turns hugging their sister.

Zylon moved to her. *If any of them get out of line, I will rip them to shreds.*

They won't get a chance.

And I knew she was right. They all grew stronger from the transformation. As part of Kane's pack, they were my family too. Now that they were half vampire, I could feel them through Kane. They were all strong, but I could sense Zandra's power through the connection, and it burned in waves through her veins.

∞

The next night, Zeb and his brothers burst through the estate entryway. They filled the den with their great bodies, and Zeb strode to his sister's side. *The berserkers are gathered twenty miles from here in an open field. It looks as if they are preparing to attack us with all the remaining flesh-eating contingent.*

How many do you speculate are gathered, Zeb? Kane moved to Zandra's side.

I stood up, alert and ready, from my bed next to the fire.

All of them led by Matteo and Paolo. Zeb grumbled. *A few hundred.*

I padded over to Kane. *What if the challenge isn't accepted? These creatures have no honor. Why wouldn't they just try to wipe us out?*

Zandra spoke before Kane could answer. *We have prevailed before. What choice do we have? We go to challenge or die fighting.* Zandra gritted her teeth. She had prepared for battle in a simple white shift that she could shake off. Her bare feet squeaked on the planked mahogany floor as she rushed across it and out the front door.

We all followed suit with vampire speed and were upon the horde of flesh eaters within mere minutes.

Zandra stopped on the small hill above the gathering.

As we had been forewarned, several hundred berserkers milled about in an open field. Their numbers had dwindled since our numerous battles with them. Matteo and Paolo Ricci stood tall among them. Both carried the baring of leadership. They both had stripped bare to the waist in preparation of their transformation. Others discarded clothing and readied themselves for a fight.

Zandra's voice rang out above their chatter.

"I am Zandra Moretti, daughter of King Lycaon. I have been here since the existence of time."

The flesh eaters all stood and watched at attention.

"Matteo and Paolo Ricci," Zandra called out her opponents. "I challenge you for master leadership of the berserker nation! Meet me in ritual battle or show your cowardice to your packs!" Her chest heaved as her fangs dropped and her claws extended.

Matteo leaped from the middle of the pack of flesh eaters.

Kane and I stood back among the brothers so as not to distract from Zandra's purpose. I looked up at my master. *I fear for her, Master.*

As do we all. Kane's voice mingled with those of the brothers in my head.

Matteo glared at Zandra and cried out, "I accept your challenge. Now you will die."

Wow. No preamble? No posturing? Kane cocked his hip and rubbed his chin.

Matteo's bones cracked transforming to wolf. His pants ripped. He grew in stature to some eight feet with fangs and claws extended.

Zandra ripped away her shift and crouched. The bones in her body crunched and morphed faster than Matteo's. She grew to ten feet. Her wolf hair now a combination of black, brown, and white. Her golden eyes filled with blood. Sharp claws descended from her fingers and toes, and she sprang down the hill before she had completely transformed.

They met head-on at the bottom of the hill and tumbled over each other while claws slashed. Leaping to their back legs, they fought upright.

Each blow that Matteo delivered with giant clawed paws to Zandra's face, arms, and back immediately healed.

A solid swipe of her claws took off a large chunk from Matteo's shoulder. He howled in pain. She spun at unbelievable speed and took a bite out of his other shoulder. He growled and tried to tear out her eyes and throat, but she bent back and leaped over the top of him by walking up his chest and using his head as a springboard.

Kane looked at me and smiled. *She plays with him now. He is no match for her.*

Matteo whirled and caught her left side above the waist with his right paw. Black blood spurted onto the ground.

Her brothers collectively gasped. My body shivered and fear rose within Kane and me.

Zandra roared. The healing wound served as a wakeup call not to underestimate Matteo. She spun, lifted her left leg, and sucker punched him in the stomach.

The berserker growled and staggered backward holding his middle.

Sidestepping, Zandra went down on one arm and spun her feet against his legs, knocking him to his back. She jumped on his chest with both knees, and his grunting and screaming brought his followers forward.

Zeb ran halfway down the hill, followed by Zylon and the other brothers.

Kane shot a message to them. *Use your mind control to stop them in their tracks.*

Zeb and his brothers in one collective thought mentally shouted. *You will not move. You will let this ritual fight play out.*

The berserkers hesitated, but surged forward.

Again, the brothers struggled to get control. They grasped each other's hands, made a circle, and mentally shouted again. *You will not move. You will honor this ritual fight and let it play out without interference.*

Just as the horde of flesh eaters reached Matteo and Zandra, they stopped in their tracks and didn't move a muscle. They stood in a trancelike stupor.

Zandra took Matteo by the throat with one paw and banged his head on the rocky ground over and over with her other.

He struggled against her, biting at the hairy paw that held his throat.

Zandra let go and delivered a heavy blow to Matteo's face. "Do you yield your leadership of the flesh eaters?" She growled the words rather than spoke them.

The sound of it made my hair stand on end.

"Never!" Matteo half-growled and partly screamed. He fought to push her off, but failed in his weakened state.

Zandra swiped the side of his face, ripping away an eye and an ear.

"Do you yield leadership?" She growled again.

Matteo's screams filled the air.

The brothers held the berserkers in a trance. They continued to hold hands. Their bodies shook with the strain of holding back so many enemies.

Matteo reached up to touch Zandra, but his arm fell to the ground as she ripped it off.

"Do you yield?" Her words were like gravel on a dirt road.

Bleeding and dying, Matteo gasped. "I yield. End me."

Zandra leaped up, lifted Matteo over her head, and ripped his head from his body. She twirled and threw it at Paolo's feet.

Kane sent a telepathic message to the brothers. *Release them.*

The berserkers finally blinked collectively and stood in shock at the site of their leader's head at the feet of Paolo.

Zandra faced him, morphing into her human form as she did. "Do you yield the right of leadership from your brother Matteo to me, Paolo?"

He roared and lunged at her. She dodged him, backed away, and morphed again. This time she transformed into a red demon that reminded me of a hellhound. Red flames shot from her body and bloody eyes. Long, saber-tooth-tiger-like fangs bit into Paolo's berserker arm as he attempted to transform as well. Her flaming body shot fire up his arm, and he screamed in agony. He staggered backward, rolled on the ground, and beat out the flames.

Kane and I were amazed that she had inherited Kane's ability to change into other forms. Kane smiled at me. *She is impressive.*

Tired of the fighting, she grabbed him from the ground faster than I could follow, pressed him to her fiery body, and covered him in flames.

His screams shot upward into the air over his cowering pack. Her abilities overwhelmed them. In one swift movement, she lifted Paolo over her head and snapped his burning body in half. Dropping him on the ground, she ripped off his burning head and threw it into his pack. They scattered and howled.

Zandra whirled and faced the spread-out assembly. She morphed back to her human form. Her naked body dripped of Matteo's blood. "I am Zandra Moretti. Daughter of King Lycaon, the original of our kind. Who would challenge me as your leader?"

Not one of them came forward.

Zandra waited as the seconds ticked by. When she was satisfied no other challenger would step forward, she spread her arms with her palms facing them and shouted, "Then bend a knee!"

The remaining berserker pack knelt in unison and bowed their heads.

She pivoted back toward us and looked up into Kane's eyes. *That should resolve this problem for the time being.*

He smiled his approval while her brothers surrounded her and covered her with hugs and kisses.

I wondered how long the flesh eaters would remain subservient to Zandra or if she and her brothers would have to put them to sleep at some point.

EPISODE SEVEN

THE SERAPH BLADE

A seraph blade engulfed by heavenly fire and infused with angels' spirits is lethal to a succubus or incubus. Kane revealed his extensive research to Zandra and me several nights after the now vampire-Lycan hybrid had brought the berserkers under her control.

We stood in the kitchen as we refreshed ourselves on the store of human blood he kept in steady supply.

But she is immortal. It won't kill Lilith. Zandra polished off her large glass of AB Neg and set it on the counter.

No, but it will rid us of Samil and Lilith and send them back from where they came. Kane rubbed his smooth chin and finished his glass of O Neg, my favorite and his.

The daylight hours had passed uneventfully while we rested and James and Zandra guarded Kane. He'd spent every night pouring through tomes of ancient manuscripts until he found an answer.

How do we get a seraph blade? I licked my chops to capture the last drop of blood on my lips.

Let me guess, Zandra teased. *Seraph means a member of the highest order of angels. So, we'd need to get a seraph blade from an angel?*

An angel? Like Seth and Mathias, you told me about, Kane? Tell Zandra about them. I want to know more. I jumped up and put my paws on his broad shoulders and licked a drop of blood from the corner of his mouth.

He laughed and pushed me down. *Not exactly. But, yes, angels like Seth and Mathias are involved, but I'll tell you more about them later. This entire process is complicated.*

How is it more complicated? Zandra and I simultaneously questioned.

We need to find a Shadowhunter to locate and invoke the blade's power. Kane moved to the doorway between the kitchen and the den and motioned us to follow.

He abruptly changed the subject which frustrated me. *How are you feeling, Zandra?*

Hmm… fighting back fits of rage and wanting to rip out a throat or two, but hanging in. She smiled sweetly causing Kane to laugh.

And your brothers? He arched his eyebrows at her as they both sat in the matching chairs in front of the fireplace.

I settled into my bed next to the fire.

The same, although the poor animals in the forest are taking the brunt of their rage and urges.

Where are they? I sneezed and looked up at her.

Spending time with the berserkers, showing them our ways of behaving and dealing with combative situations. They left right after dawn this morning. She looked Kane in the eyes. *Stop stalling. What do we need to do to find and use the seraph blade?*

Kane sat forward and rubbed his chin. *Before the blade can be used, a Shadowhunter must name it to invoke its power. Any angel's name, except for Raziel's, can be called upon.*

Why not Raziel? I sat up.

Kane got up and started to pace. He appeared to grow more and more like his sire Brogio as time passed. He wore less brilliant clothing, which he had always adored. He appeared more in black and dark-blue clothes. His sire had always dressed in nothing but black. He had become more serious and less carefree. When Kane was distracted, I could hear his other progeny in the background of his mind... Mia tittering over a dress. Marco resisting the urge to take a human life. Being the father of a nation of beings must be a heavy burden.

Because Raziel created the Shadowhunters who are hybrid angels/humans. Kane sat back and placed one booted foot across his knee.

Hybrid angel-humans? The wonders of this vampire life always surprised me. I settled back down on my bed.

Kane, always one to share his knowledge of history and legends, launched into an answer to my question. *Shadowhunters are also known as Nephilim. They're a secretive race of beings who are humans born with angel blood. They have fought demons and lived in a Shadow World for more than a thousand years. They've created their own civilization within human society. They are dedicated to keeping the peace in the Shadow World and hide it from everyday life while protecting the inhabitants of both.*

How do you know about them? I quizzed.

Kane laughed. *I was one of the demons they used to chase after.*

How does the blade work? Zandra sat forward and placed her elbows on her knees.

Within the Shadowhunter community, it is often believed that when one of them names a seraph blade, the blade becomes engulfed by heavenly fire and the spirit of the angel named is infused in it as well.

Yes, Zandra's eyes searched Kane's face, *but do we plunge the knife into Lilith and Samil to get rid of them?*

Something like that.

I stood up from my bed again and walked over to Kane's chair. *Time is awasting. We need to find a Shadowhunter to help us. Or, do you know one?*

Zandra stood and came to Kane's side as well. *We need to get going before Lilith tries another assault on us, and especially you.*

To answer Moon's question, I know a Shadowhunter called Magnum.

How do you know Magnum? I searched my master's face for answers.

Despite their ancestry, Shadowhunters are mortal and vulnerable to aging and dying. But their angelic blood gives them special abilities to achieve beyond those of normal humans.

I grew impatient. *That doesn't answer my question.*

Okay. In the 1900s, Magnum believed I was a dangerous demon and needed to be destroyed. We fought, but like I said, he was vulnerable. I spared his life to show him that I wasn't evil. He's probably never forgotten it. He's somewhat of a moral creature.

Zandra sat on the arm of his chair and placed her hand on Kane's shoulder. *So, he will help us?*

Or kill us in the process.

Oh, great. Zandra threw up her hands. *Now I'll have to kill an angel-man.*

Kane took one of her hands from the air and held it. *Most likely not. I'll prevent it.*

Where can we find Magnum? I nudged Kane's arm and put my head under his other hand.

In the Silent City beneath the New York City Marble Cemetery in Manhattan.

Where's Manhattan? I twisted my head from side to side in a curious pose.

New York City.

Where's New York City?

In the United States. He smirked, continuing to tease me.

Where's—

It's another country, Moon. Zandra laughed.

So not far? I stretched, anticipating another car ride.

Not exactly. Kane scratched me behind the ears.

It's across the ocean from us, Moon, Zandra clarified.

I let out a whimper. *I see another coffin ride in the belly of an airplane in my future.*

He rubbed my head. *It can't be helped, girl. It's the only solution I have right now of eliminating Lilith.*

EPISODE EIGHT

MAGNUM

I dwelled on my hatred of Lilith during the first part of the flight in a coffin in the back of the airplane since we had to travel during daylight. I hadn't realized that Zandra was as wealthy as Kane. She insisted we use her private jet to travel to New York. Kane had ordered his own to make my travel easier, but it was being custom-built and wasn't ready for this trip.

Zandra enjoyed the luxury seating of the aircraft and took regular glasses of blood from her compelled pilot and crew. Kane and I escaped the coffins when the sun set. Once we had consumed our share of human blood, Kane filled us in on Seth and Mathias.

Seth was an angel who fell to Earth for the love of a human woman. In the process, he became a white witch. His story is too long to share right now, but while he resided on Earth, God the Father sent another angel, Mathias, to guard over him. You see, God favored Seth and was broken-hearted when he chose to fall from grace.

I squirmed on the expansive leather seat across from Kane and Zandra to get more comfortable. *When you used to tell my hybrid siblings and me stories about our biological father, Snow Blood, I remember you said Mathias came to Earth in the form of a horse.*

A horse? Zandra's voice reflected her surprise.

Not just any horse. Kane's voice indicated his admiration of Mathias. *A Friesian with long mane and tail, feathers that covered his hoofs, and wings. He said that he chose that form because it pleased him.*

How did you come to know the two of them, Kane? Zandra scooted closer to him on the love-seat-like recliner they shared.

Seth lived in Wolfville near Brogio's estate. I practiced the white arts of witchcraft, and we became friends. He helped me out with a problem. Then, Seth got into some trouble... a lengthy story... and Brogio, Selene, Snow Blood, and I helped him out. Because of what he had experienced and because God loved Seth so much, he was granted his return to heaven. To show his gratitude to us for our help, he and Mathias convinced God the Father to grant Brogio and those he loved their humanness again. That was what Brogio had yearned for. Both of you know that I declined to take back my humanness so that I could continue to acquire knowledge, which is my great passion.

I couldn't help but ask. *Do you regret that decision?*

Not for a moment. If I had, I wouldn't have had the relationships that developed with the two of you. I might have missed out on the opportunity to work with my current mentor, Elon Musk.

You mentioned him once before. Do you mean the founder and CEO of SpaceX? Zandra expressed her surprise.

Yes, the very one. I am supposed to work on a project for him, but have been too busy to begin since Moon and I returned from Los Angeles.

I couldn't help but brag to Zandra about my sire. *Besides being an apprentice to Leonardo da Vinci at the time he became vampire, he has worked with great minds through the ages, like Shakespeare, Tesla, and Einstein.*

Before Zandra could relate how impressed she was, the attendant announced that we would be landing and should buckle up. *Perfect timing! I eagerly awaited a run to stretch my legs.*

Because it was nighttime at the Teterboro private airport in New Jersey, I looked forward to an immediate escape from the jet.

After we landed and Zandra dismissed the flight crew, the three of us downed a few more bags of O Neg, which I lapped up with greed.

I shook with vigor and pranced up and down the aisle of the airplane. *I want to go for a run.*

Kane patted my head. *If memory serves me, a large field of green grass runs parallel to the air strip. It's after midnight. Most of the activity should be cleared out.* He nodded and pointed to the airplane entryway, and I sprinted out and down the stairs.

Traces of acidity assaulted my nose, and I sneezed. Looking around, all appeared quiet, so I headed toward the field, dodged parked airplanes, and ran like the wind to stretch my legs. I inhaled the night air for signs of prey. Finding nothing but a few birds, I scooted back to the plane just as a black stretch limousine with blacked-out windows pulled up beside the jet.

I see James has arranged for transportation, I noted as I rejoined Kane and Zandra on the tarmac.

Of course. Kane nodded as the driver, another one of his mysterious, black-clad servants opened the door for us.

I still think it's cutting it close to try and get to the Shadowhunter's clave tonight. Zandra's eyes flashed with concern at Kane as she sat down in the rear seat next to him.

I took a long seat next to the window so that I could stretch out.

Kane pointed to the dark-tinted windows. *That's why we have these.*

So, you'd just take your rest inside this limo if the sun rises before we can return to the plane? Zandra glanced at the windows.

Exactly.

Kane opened the small refrigerator and pulled out three more bags of human blood. *This should keep us going.*

After we had enjoyed the delicious treat, I nosed the window marveling at how I could see New Jersey and later New York City, but people on the outside of the limo couldn't see in. It seemed like enough time to lope around Kane's entire property before the driver pulled up and stopped at the Marble Cemetery.

"*Wait here,*" Kane commanded to the driver as he opened the door for us. My master reached into the small refrigerator again and pulled out a small vial that he placed in his black jacket pocket.

Jumping out of the car, he reached in and helped Zandra out, and I jumped to the ground after her.

Kane opened the large entrance gate and strode directly to the statue of an angel holding a stone cup.

He reached into his pocket and pulled out the vial. *This is a small sample of Magnum's blood. He gave it to me in case I ever needed to contact him.* He poured the contents of the vial into the stone cup.

The statue immediately moved backward revealing an opening with stone steps downward. Zandra and I followed as Kane descended the stairs. It appeared to be an underground city with multiple levels. The first level housed a library-like archive filled with scrolls, tablets, books, maps, and numerous objects of the like.

Kane stopped and looked longingly at all the treasures he might uncover there. He turned away reluctantly and followed the hallway and descended to another level that opened into a square pavilion. Its center held a black-and-white-veined basalt table that looked like a meeting place. In front of it was a larger black marble square on the floor engraved with a parabolic design of silver stars. *This is the council chamber of the Shadowhunters, Moon.*

Kane pointed to a sword hanging above the stars engraved on the floor.

Is that the seraph blade? Zandra asked.

No, Kane's thoughts reflected reverence. *It's the Soul-Sword they call the Mortal Sword. Seraph blades are the main weapons of the Shadowhunters. They are made of adamas.*

What's that? I walked around in front of Kane.

A heavenly metal.

"Why are you here, Kane? Why have you brought demons with you?"

The deep voice startled me. I spun around to see a tall, slender, but muscular man with blond curly hair, angular cheekbones, and piercing blue eyes standing behind us. He wore form-fitting black leather pants and a black tank top. His arms were tattooed with the symbols that Kane had described as runes. He wore a military-style belt. A dagger hung from it.

He leaped from the floor and agilely landed in front of Kane. He unsheathed the ordinary-looking blade from his belt.

"No need for that, Magnum." Kane held out his hand. "This is Zandra. She is a vampire-Lycan hybrid. Moon here is vampire as well. They are part of my family and mean neither you nor any other human harm."

Magnum's blue eyes settled on me. "Curious. A hybrid wolf that's kindred to you?"

"Yes, I am her sire."

His curious eyes lingered on me for a moment. Turning back to Kane, he sheathed the blade. "I once told you never to enter our city accompanied by anyone else, especially demons. Since you've so casually ignored my instructions and obviously used my blood to enter our city, I assume you are here to collect the favor I owe you."

Favor? I moved closer to Kane.

Quiet, Moon. "I have a problem, yes, and in exchange for sparing your life, I would like to collect on it. Lilith and a wolf she calls Samil have singled us out."

"Ah… the original succubus. Samil you say? Satan more likely." Magnum backed away and pointed at chairs next to the table. "Sit."

Kane hesitated. "What about your brothers? Can we expect to be overrun by other Nephilim?"

"Perhaps. They know I have it under control, but their curiosity may get the better of them." Magnum sat and pointed again to the chairs.

Kane and Zandra sat, and I moved around between them and sat on my haunches.

"They have targeted you three? Then, what do you need from me? My gift of sight? Ah, wait, no. You need my seraph blade."

"Yes, is it possible for me to wield it?" Kane leaned forward and looked into Magnum's eyes.

"No, because the blade is infused with angel fire, night creatures can't handle it." He sighed.

"What about me? I am a day walker." Zandra leaned toward the Shadowhunter.

Magnum appeared to lean away from her. "Uh, no. You might walk in daylight, but you are a demon creature."

Zandra frowned and tried to shake off her disappointment.

"Then, Magnum, I must ask you to help us by using your blade on Lilith and Samil." Kane stood and began to pace.

Magnum stood and laughed. "You're wasting your favor. I will be delighted to rid the worlds of those abominations. However, I must warn you. They are immortals. My blade may not do the trick."

Kane stopped in front of the angel-man and fixed him with his dark eyes. "But you will try, right?"

"With pleasure."

A warning ripple shot through my spine. I rotated to see tattooed Nephilim, both men and women, peering at us from behind columns and statues in the hall. They resembled Magnum. The Nephilim had deftly crept in and watched us with unblinking eyes. They unnerved me.

Zandra stood and surveyed them. Her claws dropped from her fingers.

Nothing to worry about, Kane shot at us. *Magnum's word is golden. They are just curious as he said they would be.*

Zandra and I relaxed as one by one they retreated.

I began to feel the sun starting to climb the sky even though we were underground.

I know, Moon. "Magnum, we need to go to our rest. We will return at sunset tomorrow."

"I will be ready, Kane." Magnum handed Kane a vial of his blood. "Meet me here in this chamber then."

∞

I opened my eyes as the last rays of the sun sunk below the horizon. The day had been passed without issues, other than I found the seats in the limo not to my liking. Kane sat up and removed more human blood bags from the car refrigerator.

Zandra, who had apparently slept on Kane's shoulder, leaned forward and stretched.

After partaking the wonderful nectar, we exited the limo as the driver opened it for us.

The three of us marched toward the familiar statue and entered the same way we had the night before. Magnum awaited us in the Council Chamber.

We made a circle around the Shadowhunter who drew his blade.

"I need to call upon the power of an angel's name to access the power of the blade." Magnum held out the blade in front of him. "Do you have the name of an angel in mind?"

"Yes." Kane nodded.

"Does this angel have a connection to you?"

Again, Kane responded in the affirmative.

The Shadowhunter gave Kane a knowing look. "The louder I call the angel's name, the stronger the blade. So, don't be alarmed if I appear to be shouting."

Magnum smiled. "You might want to cover your ears." He yelled one word: "SETH!"

His scream attacked my ears like nothing I had ever felt. It pierced my inner ears with excruciating pain. As I fell to the floor trying to press against it to blot out the sound, I saw Kane and Zandra bending double with their hands covering their ears.

My ears rang as if I'd gone through an explosion. I struggled to my feet only to be blinded by the glowing light from the ordinary blade as it grew in length. It became translucent, almost crystal clear with shimmering golden lights piercing through it. I winced with more pain.

The unfurling of wings caused me to twirl around. I froze in my tracks. The most beautiful creature I had ever seen stood in the room with us. His clothing was solid white and indistinct. Piercing blue eyes and flawless skin framed by long, golden hair hung to his waist. I thought him more magnificent than Selene, something unimaginable to me.

Magnum bowed and held out the blade to what had to be an angel.

I thought, *Could this be Seth?*

Yes, Kane shot back to me.

"I hereby name this blade 'Seth.'" Magnum's deep voice echoed in the chamber.

Seth stepped forward and wrapped one glowing hand around the blade. The knife lengthened even more. The metal glowed a translucent white. Colors swirled. His voice and the blessing it carried rang like music through my ears. "May heavenly fire be your strength. This blade called Seth shall strike down those who carry evil in their hearts."

Zandra and I stood back. I could feel that she had become as awestruck as I.

Kane took a step forward and held out his hand to the angel who smiled at my master. His image gradually disappeared.

Magnum's eyes touched each of ours. "We are ready to face Lilith and Samil."

∞

"Does Magnum need to return to Italy with us, or can we confront these demons anywhere?" Zandra voiced her question as we all ascended the stairs to the outside.

With a wave of his arm, Magnum magically opened the sliding door to the surface. "Once we are out of the sanctity of our clave, we can encounter her anywhere."

As I stepped onto the cemetery ground, my hackles rose. The familiar pull on my movements rippled through me. *She is here!*

At that moment, Samil leaped from behind the angel statue toward me. Magnum swept his arm, and the opening to the Shadowhunters' city slammed shut.

Kane whirled and flung Samil mid-leap.

Lilith's laughter rose in the air. She glided toward us. Her long, wavy red hair swirled around her face and arms, and her glowing green eyes fixated on Magnum. "Shadowhunter, do you really think your blade will destroy me?"

She rose above the ground, and her beauty dissolved into a screaming she-creature that could only be described as an abomination. Sharp points grew out of her spine. Fangs dropped below her chin and dripped with saliva. Her hair became a tangle of hissing snakes, and her skin turned a motley gray. Sunken cheeks accentuated black eyes that receded into her skull. Clawlike talons grew from her fingers and bare toes. Before I could blink, she latched onto Magnum and attempted to draw his angelic soul from his body. He staggered back, and Kane grabbed handfuls of her writhing snake hair and yanked her off him.

Teeth and claws slashing, Samil spun away from me and tackled Zandra. She pushed him off, and he landed on me. I bit into his neck and ripped out a large chunk of it. I jumped back expecting him to foam at the mouth and die. To my surprise, his body trembled for a moment, but he shook it off and went after Zandra again. *He warned me my venom would not affect him.*

Behind me I heard a scuffle. Kane went flying over my head. I whirled around in time to see Magnum drive his angelic sword into Lilith's heart.

The demon's screams pierced the air, and she swirled round and round. The sound of her voice took all of us to the ground in agony. Even Samil hit the ground and howled. The more she swirled, the louder Lilith's screams grew until she imploded. Green ashes floated to the barren ground and soaked into the earth.

I sprang up just in time to see Zandra rise and hit Samil so hard that he flew across several tombstones and smashed into a mausoleum.

Magnum and Kane both leaped over the tombstones and were about to land on top of the wolf demon when the unfurling of wings froze them in midair.

I tried to move next to Zandra but had no power to do so. Everyone, including Samil, was frozen. Time stood still.

The same beautiful angel called Seth appeared next to the most magnificent horse. All black, his wingspan must have reached six feet on either side of his shoulders. His long mane hung past his shoulders. His thick tail touched the ground, and hairy feathers covered his hooves. Mathias was every bit as Kane had described.

Even though Magnum didn't move, the angel blade glowed more brightly than before. The two angels appeared to have stepped out of the weapon.

They strolled to the wolf and surrounded him with bright light that brought pain to my eyes.

The wolf began to shimmer. The brighter the light, the more the wolf glowed until Samil threw back his head and a flood of black soot streamed from his throat. It rose in a cloud, flipped downward, and plummeted to the Earth where it soaked into the ground. The dazed wolf staggered to his feet, backed away from us, and yapped as he ran into the darkness.

My body was released as were that of Kane and Magnum who completed their leap from the air to the ground. Zandra swirled around. Her face reflected shock. "What the... hell?"

Seth turned to Kane. His voice again chimed like music. "Lilith has not ceased to exist. She has just retreated."

Mathias stomped the ground and snorted.

Kane approached the angels. "What did you do to the wolf?"

A strong, deep voice filled my head.

The wolf was an innocent possessed by Satan. We merely sent "Samil" back to where he belongs. The Friesian horse angel's head moved up and down as he transmitted his message to all of us.

Kane stood before the angelic pair. He bowed his head and spoke with a soft voice. "Once again the two of you have come to my rescue. Thank you."

Zandra and I joined Kane to show our gratitude.

"Thank Magnum." Seth looked back at the Shadowhunter who stood next to the statue of the angel and the entrance to his clave. "It is his power that brings us here. You now must deal with the succubus. Magnum knows what must come next."

Both angels began to fade.

Thank you! Zandra and I sent a mental message to them.

You are born of Snow Blood and Kane, Moon. We are watching.

Their words sent shivers down my spine, and Kane's eyes locked with mine for a moment.

Even though we are creatures of the night, I guess they think we still have value to God the Father. A faint smile crossed Kane's lips.

Zandra looked to Magnum. "What did the angels mean by 'Magnum knows what must come next?'"

Magnum sheathed his weapon which had reverted to a dull dagger. "We can't kill an immortal, but we can cause her to become trapped and powerless." He looked pointedly at me. "Seth and Mathias let me see how your biological sire worked with Hades to trap and isolate Hecate, the goddess of witches."

Kane took two long strides to stand before Magnum. "Tell us what we need to do."

EPISODE NINE

TRAPPED AND ISOLATED

Magnum sat with Kane and Zandra in the den at the Tuscany estate. I lay listening to them in my bed next to the fireplace, trying to overcome the trauma of once again traveling in a coffin across the ocean on a private jet. Odd as it may seem, I found being in an enclosure like a coffin more terrifying than anything else that I had experienced in my kindred life. I forced myself to get over it and focus on their conversation.

"The only thing that Lilith loves more than being a succubus," Magnum leaned toward my master who sat opposite him while Zandra perched on the arm of Kane's chair, "is her own reflection."

"Well," Zandra shrugged, "she is quite beautiful in her human form."

Kane looked up at the she-wolf and smiled. "She can't hold a candle to you."

Magnum, a no-nonsense kind of guy, ignored Kane's remark and leaned back in his chair.

"Because she is so drawn to her reflection, we can render her powerless."

Kane reached up and stroked Zandra's arm. "By trapping her in a mirror."

"Exactly."

"What?" Zandra clasped Kane's hand to her arm. "How would that work? She's intelligent and most likely knows her weaknesses."

Magnum stood and stretched his long body. "That's why we'll use an infinity mirror that will reflect Kane's image to her. She'll be able to see her own reflection beside Kane."

I sat up in alarm. *You don't mean that my master would be in the mirror and vulnerable to Lilith, do you?*

The Shadowhunter smiled at me. "Always thinking of how to protect your master, aren't you, Moon." He looked back at Kane. "The infinity mirror will allow me to project Kane's recorded image using rear projection from behind it. Once she steps in, we will make sure she is trapped."

I lay back down and sighed.

Along with Magnum, James was tasked with gathering the equipment needed for the attempt to trap the succubus. I noted a frown on the manservant's face as he leaned against the wall while Kane and Magnum discussed the necessary equipment. They were to go during the daylight hours into Florence to secure everything.

Zeb returned just before sunrise. His unannounced entrance into the house caused a stir. Magnum leaped from his chair, drew his seraph blade, and went after Zandra's oldest brother.

Kane swerved around the Shadowhunter and put out a hand before he could reach Zeb. "Stop! This is Zandra's brother."

The hybrid brother had begun to morph before Magnum reached him.

Zandra leaped over all their heads and landed in front of her brother to shield him.

Magnum halted and raised an eyebrow at Kane. "How many hybrid demons have you befriended?"

Zeb's husky voice responded, "Not befriended. Sired."

Magnum took a step back. "Why would you infest the world with such powerful demons? How can you ask me to help you with Lilith when you are guilty of producing those just as bad as she?"

Kane pushed back the Shadowhunter and pointed to the chair. "Let me explain. Don't judge until you understand."

While Kane filled in Magnum, I followed Zeb and Zandra into the dining room, where James had perceived everyone's hunger and laid out a meal of AB Neg. The man was uncanny.

"How goes it with the berserkers?" Zandra asked after draining her glass of nectar.

Saliva dripped from my jowls as James set down a bowl of O Neg for me.

"It's good." Zeb gulped the rare blood with gusto. "Our brothers have everything under control. The flesh eaters are docile enough and have sworn allegiance to you and to us."

"Good news. We needed it. Listen, I need you to return to our brothers. We're dealing with another threat, and it's best you're not involved." Zandra placed her hand on her brother's arm.

He covered it with one of his large, paw-like hands. Looking into her eyes, he searched their depths. "Are you sure?"

"Yes. Now go. I love you." She hugged him.

He wrapped both arms around her, lifted her off the floor, and gave her a bear hug. "Me too." He rubbed his eyes, spun around, and left without a word to Kane.

James followed behind the hybrid brother and stopped next to our master. "The sun comes, sir."

Kane rose from his chair as Zandra joined him.

Magnum seemed appeased with Kane's explanation of the hybrids. He stood as well.

"James, you will accompany Magnum to Rome?"

The servant bowed his head. "Sir, I have never disobeyed any command you have ever given me, but please don't ask me to leave you unprotected during your rest. I fear the she-demon will return. Can't the Shadowhunter gather the necessary equipment?"

James' words shocked me.

Kane raised his eyebrows and just stared at his manservant.

"He's right, Kane," Magnum offered. "I am capable of getting what we need. It is best he stays here during your rest when you are most vulnerable."

Zandra stepped up. "Wait a minute. Are you suggesting I'm not capable of protecting Kane and Moon during their sleep?" She glared at James.

"Not at all, madam... I..."

"Enough." Kane's strong voice silenced the disagreement. He looked at Zandra. "I think you are more than capable, but I've learned to trust James' instincts. If he *feels* he needs to stay here, then he has good reason."

James bowed his head again. "Thank you, sir."

"Humph!" Zandra shook her head, but said no more about it.

Magnum headed for the door and without looking snatched up the keys that Kane tossed him. "Take the Town Car. It's large enough to hold everything."

The Shadowhunter disappeared through the door, and the rest of us headed up the stairs.

∞

In the middle of our rest, James reminded me again why he should never be underestimated.

I felt cold fingers rake my body. Startled, I tried to rise but felt sluggish. My immediate concern focused on my master.

Kane's body twitched.

Zandra shot straight up and reached for him.

A slight outline of Lilith's form hovered over him. With one arm, she backhanded Zandra in the face, knocking her out of the bed.

Before she could rise and retaliate, James tore into the shimmering form over Kane and ripped her off his master. Holding her in the air, he delivered punch after powerful punch over her face and body.

I struggled to move but knew, through my connection with Kane, Lilith held us both down.

Lilith tore free and latched onto James' shoulders while attempting to suck out his soul. As the creature did so, she let out a high-pitched scream that deafened me.

Taking her long, red hair in one hand, James yanked her away enough for Zandra to grab the blade the manservant always carried and plunge it into the demon's heart.

Lilith's withering screams filled the room, and once again, green smoke and ashes lingered where she had last been.

Freed from her magical hold on me, I leaped up snarling with my teeth bared.

Kane, as sluggish as I had been, sat up and shook his head. Blinking, he stared at Zandra and James, both of whom looked battle-worn. Lilith sucked the energy from all with whom she came in contact.

He sighed. "You have to hand it to her. She's persistent."

I walked over his legs and licked his face.

He rubbed my head and opened an arm to Zandra to join him as he looked at James. "Thank you, both. She knows when I'm most vulnerable, but you'd think she'd get it that the two of you aren't going to relent either."

I licked his face even harder. *I tried, Master, but my link to you rendered me useless.*

Kane reached out and pulled me to his other side and hugged Zandra and me to him. "Good thing your hybrid strength allows you to resist her power, Zandra." Lying back down, he continued to hold us both as he closed his eyes and resumed his rest.

I watched as James leaned back with his arms crossed on the bedroom wall. The strength he possessed remained a mystery to me. His ever-alert eyes stared into the darkness.

I closed my eyes and felt safe in the knowledge that James with his precognitive sense watched over us.

∞

Magnum awaited us in the den when we arose from our rest. The equipment he had secured sat in the large foyer.

After we all took sustenance, Magnum videoed my master to project his image into the mirror to entice Lilith.

Zandra and I stayed back in the kitchen with James so as not to be a distraction. We watched him as he cut meat with his parrying blade. I recalled how he always used the blade when he cooked. It had become his all-purpose knife for both the kitchen and for fighting demons when a sword wasn't handy.

Zandra took the opportunity to sate her curiosity (and mine) about James. "Tell me about yourself, James. How long have you been devoted to Kane?"

James lowered his eyes, not meeting hers. "I came to Kane's sire, Brogio, when I was a teenager. After Brogio regained his soul and his humanness, he gifted me to my master. So, I have been in servitude to them a total of twenty-five years."

"But why? It's almost as if you sold your soul into bondage." Zandra perched on one of the bar stools surrounding the counter of the black-and-white kitchen. She put her elbows on the counter and placed her chin on her knuckles.

I sat back on my haunches and awaited his answer.

"For immortality. I pledged my life to Brogio in exchange for the gift of eternal life. When he could no longer gift it to me, he passed me to the one who could." James busied himself by cleaning up the spotless kitchen.

I could tell that talking about himself unnerved him.

Zandra pressed him further. "So, how long do you have to remain his servant before he makes you kindred to him?"

James stopped rubbing a hole in the counter and lifted his chin slightly. "Whenever he deems that the time is right. But it makes no matter. My life will always be bound to him whether I am a human or vampire."

He is like me without the benefits.

I communicated my thought to the she-wolf. *Likewise.*

Zandra smiled at me. *Except, I'm enjoying the benefits that I am receiving.*

If I'd had hands, I would have put them over my eyes. *That's too much information, Zandra.*

She laughed out loud, and James' face flushed red with embarrassment.

"No, I'm not laughing at you, James. It's Moon. She cracks me up at times."

Because James could now hear my mental conversations, I knew he had grown uncomfortable being discussed.

James gave me a quick glance, and his lips almost smiled. "The hybrid has a mind of her own, but she is ever-faithful and would die for our master as I would. She loves him as I do. She is the most noble of creatures."

Zandra nodded in agreement, and I felt pride and sat up straight trying to look as regal as possible.

Getting back on track, Zandra continued her questions of James. "How did you develop such strength as a human and learn to fight as you do? And do you have the gift of sight?"

James shrugged. "You ask many questions, ma'am. I learned from watching my master, Brogio, and his first blood son, whom I now serve."

"And your exceptional strength?"

"Training over time. Brogio once gave me a small taste of his blood. It strengthened me. It gave me some precognitive abilities. I sense things rather than see them." James bowed to her and left the room. I assumed to avoid her further questions.

I stared at her, and she looked back at me. *What? Don't tell me you're not curious about him too.*

I snorted. *Could you not sense his discomfort at all the personal questions?*

Yes, but I wanted to know. Zandra smiled and winked at me.

You aren't subtle about what you want, are you? I took the opportunity to scratch my right ear and secretly appreciated that James' mystery had been partially explained.

No. Everyone will always know what I'm thinking and what I want. Aren't you the pot calling the kettle black? This time she snorted.

Before I could ask what that meant, Kane strolled into the kitchen. *The mirror is all set up. Magnum has requested that I make myself scarce so that when Lilith reappears she won't question if that's really me in the reflection.*

That seems pointless. Zandra faced him. She arched an eyebrow and tilted her head at him. *She senses you wherever you are. What's to say she won't go to where you are rather than where you want her to be?*

Magnum sauntered into the kitchen and looked from Kane to Zandra.

"Zandra makes a good point. Lilith will be able to sense me no matter where I am. If I leave the house, she might track me down rather than approaching the mirror. I think I'd better remain nearby." Kane searched Magnum's placid face. "What do you think?"

"As you wish. It will be a struggle, either way."

"What if she appears during the daylight hours?" Zandra touched Kane's arm.

Kane smiled. "I had automatic black metal shields installed in all the windows in the house years ago. You haven't noticed them because James hasn't activated them while you've been here. He will begin to do so before sunrise today."

Magnum and Kane worked out a scenario where Kane would slip behind the mirror whenever Lilith did appear. It would be a long shot to fool her into thinking my master hid in the reflective glass.

The night passed without incident. Several days and nights went by without signs of the succubus. We all remained in the house and just waited. I can't remember a time I enjoyed less than when waiting for Lilith to appear again. It felt like quite a cat-and-mouse game.

As Kane had anticipated, Lilith made another attempt to seduce him during daylight while we rested. The succubus' ego appeared to suppress any concern that she might encounter danger after her repeated attacks.

James, Zandra, and Magnum all sat watch in our bedroom.

I felt her presence as soon as Lilith touched him. Both my master and I struggled against her touch. Our eyes flew open. She held us both in her grip. She attempted to hold our guardians at bay. The Shadowhunter screamed Seth's name. He shattered my ears. The glow of the seraph blade pierced through my body. Its glow hovered over Lilith and Kane. My muscles released as the blade's strength drove back the demon.

Kane and I fought through the drug-like fog we experienced when awakened from our necessary daylight rest. Moving our muscles was a challenge. We pushed against the wall of required sleep. James and Zandra surrounded her shadowy figure. Magnum held Lilith at bay with his glowing angelic translucent sword.

Kane and I slid to the edge of the bed. My sire grasped the edge. Our muscles fought against us. We pulled ourselves along like beings caught in quicksand. With every ounce of strength, we pushed off the bed and down the stairs. The blackout shields kept the entryway in darkness except for the awaiting glowing trap.

Magnum released the creature just in time for her to spy Kane appearing to slide into the mirror. I stood and barked at the mirror which now held my master's reflection.

The succubus glided down the stairs and stopped before the looking glass. She glowed and materialized, fascinated with her reflection.

I could see the look of enchantment on Lilith's face as she peered into the mirror at her reflection standing next to Kane. She took a step back and looked around the room. Her eyes found mine, and I averted them and barked louder.

She took a step forward and reached out her hand to Kane's smiling reflection whose outstretched arms appeared to beckon her. She whirled around and took another step. Then another. She reached out and first let her fingers hover near the reflection of her own face, and then that of my master. She preened at her own beauty. Her fingertips touched the mirror and then retracted. She extended them again, and the mirror parted like water. She pulled back and whirled around keeping her eyes on her backside while admiring it. She turned again and reached out to both images. Her reflection appeared to enthrall her. She seemed to ignore all else.

The scene in front of me engrossed me so completely that even I didn't hear Magnum approach her. He stood behind her in silence.

So absorbed was she in her own image, she seemed not to notice Magnum place the tip of the seraph blade next to her back. In one swift movement, he skewered her with it and shoved her into the mirror. Just as quickly, he removed the blade, and it dripped of the green blood-like liquid from her body.

Lilith screamed her ire, whirled around, and made a run toward the entrance of the mirror to escape. Her anger shook the mirror and the floor upon which I stood. Before she could free herself, Kane with vampire speed dumped the mirror on the marble tile floor, and it shattered into what appeared to be a hundred pieces.

"It is done." Magnum's glowing sword dimmed and dulled.

Darkness and silence surrounded me.

"Is it permanent?" Zandra's voice called from above on the stairs.

"Until some witch, demon, or incubus figures a way to release her. As of now, she will be powerless." Magnum's voice rang through the dark entryway. His eyes glowed in fierce intensity toward Kane. "Since no other witnesses observed her entrapment, I am hopeful she will remain suffering for an eternity or more."

Kane sighed. "Thank you, Magnum. Let us speak tonight. Moon, we should return to our rest."

Feeling the malaise that weighed me down and forced me to sleep, I padded after him up the stairs. Zandra and James followed us inside the bedroom and shut the door.

As I leaped up on the bed, relief flooded through me in the knowledge that Lilith had been trapped and rendered powerless. Our life as kindred had been a never-ending challenge for survival. I couldn't help but wonder what awaited us next.

EPISODE TEN

THE END OF THE BEGINNING

I awoke as the sun slipped below the horizon. The automatic lights illuminated the dark room. The feeling of continuing dread lingered around me like flies on a rancid piece of meat.

Zandra stretched next to Kane who sat up and brushed his long hair from his eyes.

James slid out the bedroom door, and I hopped down after him.

Magnum rattled around in the kitchen helping himself to premade coffee and toasting bread. He appeared to have rested well.

James hurried to prepare glasses of human blood for my master and Zandra and a bowl for me.

I lapped the last drop of my glorious nectar from my bowl as Kane and Zandra joined us.

"Ah, Magnum," Kane marched to the Shadowhunter with his hand extended, "let me thank you properly." The two shook hands, and my master patted Magnum on the back. "I owe you."

"No," Magnum murmured. "A life for a life. We are even. I need to return to the clave."

Zandra offered, "My jet will take you."

Kane looked over his shoulder. "James? Bring the car around front."

The manservant headed off, but Kane stopped him. "Thank you, James. Those words are hollow for all that you do for me, but they are heartfelt."

James bowed his head and whispered, "Thank you, sir." He made his way to the garage.

Kane drained his prepared repast as Zandra approached the Shadowhunter.

"Thank you, Magnum, for everything." She didn't try to touch him but bowed her head slightly.

The Shadowhunter stepped back and bowed to her. "My pleasure, madam." He straightened and gave Zandra a rare smile.

His jovial action took me by surprise as his demeanor had always been so sober.

Kane moved next to the demon killer. "If you should ever need me, Magnum..."

The Shadowhunter's hand stopped my master's words. "Understand this, Kane. We are even. If I should see any of you again, I will do my sworn duty."

"You mean you will kill us?" Zandra drew to her full height.

Magnum leveled his eyes at her. "You are demons. When I leave this place, that's all you will ever be to me." He strode to the front door and disappeared from our lives.

I sat back on my haunches. *He's weird.*

No, Kane retorted. *He is a Shadowhunter.*

My master put his arm around Zandra and walked her into the den. *Thank you for all that you have done to support me, my dear. You have been spectacular.* He tried to kiss her on the cheek, but the hybrid drew away.

Something has been eating at me for some time now, and I need to get it off my chest. She faced him.

The look in her golden eyes told me this wasn't going to be pleasant. I sauntered into the room behind them and tried to make myself inconspicuous.

Do I need a glass of wine to sustain me through this? Kane raised his eyebrows at her.

Without responding, Zandra took a deep breath. *This business with Lilith has made me think about how she tried to seduce you.*

Kane remained frozen in place. *What does it matter? She didn't succeed.*

Because you told me yourself that a succubus takes the form of the person to whom the intended victim is most attracted. So, who was it that you first saw? You said she was blonde.

Zandra, Kane rolled his eyes, *why would you focus on such an unimportant detail?*

I went to my bed next to the fireplace and sat in it. I knew what was coming.

This isn't unimportant to me, Kane. You told me when you turned me that I would always love the person for whom I had feelings before I became hybrid. You know damn well that I was and am in love with you. Zandra walked to the bar, poured herself a whiskey, and drained it. She kept her back to him and asked, *So, who was she?*

Kane sighed, walked to the bar, and poured Chianti into a crystal glass. *Her name is Selene.*

The hybrid whirled around to him. *Brogio's Selene?* Zandra's eyes registered surprise. *Show me her image.*

Kane took a long sip of his wine and shrugged. I could see the beautiful image of Selene that he sent to her.

The hybrid she-wolf gasped. Her eyes narrowed. *So, I am the dark mirror image of the woman you truly love? You were attracted to me because of whom I resemble?*

I whined and lay down. This wasn't going well.

No! I am attracted to you for who you are. After Lilith's first several attempts with Selene, she only appeared as you.

Zandra ignored his comment and pressed on. *Admit that the initial attraction arose from your love for this Selene.*

Kane drained his glass and poured another. *No, I won't admit that. Lilith used my affection for Selene to trick me.*

But you are in love with Selene! A frown spread across Zandra's face.

Selene belongs to my sire, Brogio. She has loved him for an eternity. That bond is sacred to me. I would never betray his trust in me.

I felt like I was watching a tennis match as the conversation bounced back and forth.

So, I'm a substitute for the woman you really love?

Kane sighed, walked to Zandra, took her hand, and pointed to the chair next to the fireplace.

To my surprise, she sat down. He plopped down across from her.

I can't lie to you. I was first attracted to you because you resemble Selene. Until I met you, I thought her the most beautiful woman alive.

Zandra's body appeared to sink into the large, plush chair. She remained silent.

I realize now that what has kept me with you is your decency, loyalty, wit, strength, and who you are as a person. He leaned forward and searched her face.

She leaned toward him as well, her elbows on her knees. She ran a hand through her long, dark hair. *If that's true, can you move on with your life and move past this love for Selene?*

He reached across the small distance between them and took her hand. *I already have.*

I could sense the affection that he felt for Zandra run through my body.

He stood, pulled her to him, and kissed her.

I promise you that I will work hard to make this relationship work between us.

Will you remain open to love with me?

Yes.

Zandra sighed and snuggled into his chest.

I barked, and he winked at me. His private message came through loud and clear. *You will always be my number one girl, Moon.*

I will be forever faithful... A howl in the woods interrupted my message to him and alerted me to danger. I leaped up and sprinted to the front entryway. Jumping up, I pulled down on the latch and opened the door. Turning, I noted that a distracted Kane attempted to make up for lost time with Zandra.

He pushed a warning at me as I rushed out the open door to investigate the danger I perceived still surrounded us.

Be careful, Moon. Don't take any chances.

Putting my nose to the ground, I breathed in the scent of the forest. I ran and scattered frightened prey in every direction. Ignoring them, I leaped around trees, branches, and stumps and zeroed in on the musky smell of wolf. It led me deeper and deeper into the forest. I jumped over a small stream, sprinted up a low hill, and forged my way across a deep gulley. Coming up on the other side, I skidded to a stop. Shock electrified my body. I froze at the sight sitting on a pile of downed logs in front of me.

Samil.

Satan had come back to claim me. I threw back my head and howled at the full moon.

To discover Moon's fate, watch for Moon Blood, Book 4.

Thank you for reading *Moon Blood*

If you enjoyed this book and would like to give back to the author, please consider writing a review! Reviews are a tremendous help for authors. So if you were moved and enjoyed this book enough to write even one sentence of encouragement it would be a huge boon.

Want more reads from the eyes of a dog?? Get a FREE story! Join Carol McKibben's exclusive readers group for a free story, GIVEAWAYS, Advanced reader opportunities and Pre-order notifications!

Join at:

http://eepurl.com/bAuq2b

About The Author:

www.carolmckibben.com

Carol McKibben writes from the heart of a dog's eyes. Her books help support her dog rescue efforts and focus on unconditional love.

When Carol isn't saving Siberian Huskies, Labrador Retrievers, or feeding the horde of rescue dogs she and her husband Mark rehabilitate, she's out riding her sixteen-hand Frisian across the plains of Texas.

In addition to her passion for writing, she rides and competes with her dance partner Okido I.T. in Classical Dressage.

Go to www.carolmckibben.com

or https://www.facebook.com/CarolMckibbenAuthor to see beautiful pictures of her Frisian and fantastical wolves she finds on the Internet.

Other books by Carol McKibben:

<u>The Snow Blood series:</u>

Snow Blood: Season 1

Snow Blood Season 2

Snow Blood: Season 3

Snow Blood: Season 4

Snow Blood: Season 5

Kane:
The First Blood Son (prequel of the Snow Blood series)

<u>The First Blood Son series:</u>

Moon Blood: The First Blood Son series (Book 1)

Moon Blood: The First Blood Son series (Book 2)

<u>Stand alone novels:</u>

Riding Through It

Luke's Tale

Find out when the next book comes out!
Connect with Carol McKibben:

Facebook:
https://www.facebook.com/CarolMckibbenAuthor

Goodreads:
https://www.goodreads.com/author/show/4046806.Carol_McKibben

Website:
http://www.carolmckibben.com

We often update our books when grammar errors are found, so please let us know if you've found one at: stephanie@trollriverpub.com

Find Other Great Books from Troll River Publications at:

www.trollriverpub.com

www.ingramcontent.com/pod-product-compliance
Lightning Source LLC
Chambersburg PA
CBHW022131170626
46808CB00002B/937